# "I Did Not Say I Do Not Want You.

"That did not die with my love. I want to make love to you, Lisbet," he said with rough urgency. "It is the kind of wanting you wanted me to feel…a wanting without heart. Isn't it so?"

"Jaf," she pleaded.

"Tell me it is all you want!" he commanded.

As if his anguished passion were a burning brand setting her alight, now, at last, Lisbet recognized the love she had hidden deep inside. Set free by the flames of the remorse and regret that swept her, as surely as if he had burnt down a prison that held her, love stood up without disguise for the first time.

She was breathless with the discovery, and with the anguish of knowing that it had come too late.

"Tell me!"

But what she wanted to tell him, he no longer wanted to hear.

Dear Reader,

Escape the winter doldrums by reading six new passionate, powerful and provocative romances from Silhouette Desire!

Start with our MAN OF THE MONTH, *The Playboy Sheikh*, the latest SONS OF THE DESERT love story by bestselling author Alexandra Sellers. Also thrilling is the second title in our yearlong continuity series DYNASTIES: THE CONNELLYS. In *Maternally Yours* by Kathie DeNosky, a pleasure-seeking tycoon falls for a soon-to-be mom.

All you readers who've requested more titles in Cait London's beloved TALLCHIEFS miniseries will delight in her smoldering *Tallchief: The Hunter*. And more great news for our loyal Desire readers—a *brand-new* five-book series featuring THE TEXAS CATTLEMAN'S CLUB, subtitled THE LAST BACHELOR, launches this month. In *The Millionaire's Pregnant Bride* by Dixie Browning, passion erupts between an oil executive and secretary who marry for the sake of her unborn child.

A single-dad surgeon meets his match in *Dr. Desirable*, the second book of Kristi Gold's MARRYING AN M.D. miniseries. And Kate Little's *Tall, Dark & Cranky* is an enchanting contemporary version of *Beauty and the Beast*.

Indulge yourself with all six of these exhilarating love stories from Silhouette Desire!

Enjoy!

*Joan Marlow Golan*

Joan Marlow Golan
Senior Editor, Silhouette Desire

Please address questions and book requests to:
Silhouette Reader Service
U.S.: 3010 Walden Ave., P.O. Box 1325, Buffalo, NY 14269
Canadian: P.O. Box 609, Fort Erie, Ont. L2A 5X3

# The Playboy Sheikh
## ALEXANDRA SELLERS

Silhouette®

*Desire*

Published by Silhouette Books

America's Publisher of Contemporary Romance

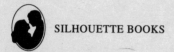 **SILHOUETTE BOOKS**

ISBN 0-373-76417-0

THE PLAYBOY SHEIKH

Visit Silhouette at www.eHarlequin.com

**Printed in U.S.A.**

## ALEXANDRA SELLERS

is the author of over twenty-five novels and a feline language text published in 1997 and still selling.

Born and raised in Canada, Alexandra first came to London, England, as a drama student. Now she lives near Hampstead Heath with her husband, Nick. They share housekeeping with Monsieur, who jumped through the window one day and announced, as cats do, that he was moving in.

What she would miss most on a desert island is shared laughter.

Readers can write to Alexandra at P.O. Box 9449, London NW3 2WH, UK, England.

for Nick
for love's sake only

# Prologue

A pair of green eyes filled the screen and smiled a challenge into the room. His stomach tightened and he caught his breath.

"This is her now," said a voice behind him.

"I know it is," said Jafar al Hamzeh. His mouth was firm with conscious control as he gazed at her. The eyes looked straight at him, into his soul.

The irises were pale green, delicately traced with darker green and russet and then bordered by a smooth, fine circle of deep emerald. The whites were pure and clear, the eyes themselves wide and slanting slightly up at the corners under straight, fair eyebrows.

He had seen those eyes close like this, and they had filled his whole world. When she had lain above him, his arms around her, and he had been consumed with a pleasure-pain that he thought would annihilate him. Or the world. He hadn't known which. Hadn't cared.

Then her eyes had been as close as this. He was aware of a deep, primitive jealousy now that the others in the room were seeing her so intimately. If he had given way to it, he would have stood up and tossed them bodily out of the studio.

The camera drew back to reveal the wide, straight forehead, smooth cheeks, the straight, slightly flat nose. Then further, and her generous, half-truculent mouth trembled into a smile. Thick, pale blond hair in a wave above her eyes fell back from her forehead and down in a luxurious tumble over one shoulder and arm.

He had lain tangled in that hair, had stroked it and threaded his fingers into it. He could feel the memory of it now on his fingertips, a sensuous silk. Its perfume was suddenly thick in his nostrils. He closed his eyes as the familiar yearning swept him.

''Very unusual beauty.''

''Real individuality...''

Behind him the voices murmured, but he scarcely heard. Onscreen, she spoke briefly, turned and walked away from the camera. She was wearing a short, tight skirt that outlined her hips, showed the slender legs. Her voice was low and resonant, as always, and amused, as it had been when he last heard it. She spoke over her shoulder, a half smile toying at the corner of her mouth, then swung her head so that her hair slid from her shoulder and tumbled down her back.

He felt it like a touch. His skin burned.

The door opened and closed, and she was gone. Just the way she had walked out of his life. A smile, a shake of the head, and the sound of a closing door.

He ached now the way he had then, for the door to

open again, for her to come back, to say she had changed her mind.

"Here's another," said a voice.

She was there again, this time in a bikini, on a beach. She was eating ice cream, totally absorbed in it, while all around her men ignored reality to watch her and dream. A man capsized a boat. His passengers waved and shouted from the water, and the lifeguard leapt to attention, but it was her that he had seen. A volleyball game collapsed in mayhem as she strolled in the sunshine, her hair blowing, her beautiful body warm with female curves. A hot dog vendor drove his cart off a pier.

*She is mine,* he told them all.

"Fabulous," murmured a voice.

There were murmurs of agreement, but Jaf said nothing. He watched her lick the cone and mime a satisfaction that was almost sexual. He had seen that look on her face before, too, but she had not been miming then. He was sure of that.

The ice cream manufacturer's logo flashed and froze onscreen above her upturned face. "Well, I don't think we could find a better addition to the harem, could we?" a man said, as if he had a choice. As if it had not been a foregone conclusion from the beginning. "I think she'd be a gift to please any sultan. How about it, Jaf?"

He smiled and nodded. Going along with the pretence. "Fine by me," he said. As if it hardly mattered to him. As if they didn't know.

She had smiled at him before she went, half mocking, challenging him. *Do your worst,* she had said.

She would see what his worst was. A gift for the sultan first, but she would be his, all his, in the end.

# One

She clung desperately to the slippery surface of the mahogany chest and rode the swell as a wave lifted her. Behind her the next wave broke with a tumbling hiss, and she gulped in air as it washed over her.

Ahead of her was the long white coastline. Beyond, miles of blinding green sea.

The sun was fierce. The salt stung her eyes. Her pale hair floated around her in the water and clung to her cheeks like rich seaweed. The long skirt of her dress, open down the front to free her legs, trailed behind her in the waves, green on green. Her legs kicked through the sparkling water, searching for a footing. As if the sea were a passionate, impatient lover, another wave rose over her and grasped her in its rough caress.

At a little distance, hidden from view behind a rocky outcrop, he sat astride a white horse, watching.

Jealousy burned in him as if he saw another man make love to her.

Her kicking foot touched ground then, and she stood upright in waist-deep water and let the wooden chest go to be pummelled and tumbled up the white sand beach by the surf.

As she struggled through the breakers, they rushed and dragged, the sea trying to pull her back into its arms. She stumbled once, and staggered, almost losing the battle, but the sea missed its moment, and she righted herself.

Still he watched, motionless, as if waiting for a sign.

The sea's froth bubbled around her as she moved, dragging her skirt back to reveal her legs and then rushing forward with it again, as if in sudden anxiety to preserve her modesty. As she came unsteadily out of the sea it danced and hissed around her slick, glowing thighs, then her knees, then her rippling calves, and finally her ankles, while her dress alternately hid and revealed her flesh.

It was an erotic and evocative striptease. His body tormented him as he imagined his hands, his mouth, his body stroking her as the waves did, reducing her to the panting exhaustion that made her breasts heave.

With a sensuous sweep, she lifted one arm to drag the long, water-soaked hair off her neck and shoulders and toss it to fall down her back. Her firm young breasts pressed against the low neckline of her dress as she moved, and her forearm showed soft and female under the green fabric.

His mount snorted and tossed its head, and he laid a hand on its neck. "Wait a little," he murmured. The horse obediently stilled.

At a point barely beyond the water's reach, in grateful, graceful exhaustion, her hands lifted high, her head fell back, and she opened her mouth with a cry of triumph and gratitude and dropped to her knees on the sand. Then she collapsed onto her back, her arms outstretched, to drink in sun and air and life.

A stronger wave rolled up the beach under her legs, lifting the skirt of her dress in a bubble and then dropping it to one side, revealing her legs again, one knee a little bent. His body hurt with the need to kiss her where the water kissed her.

The horse reacted instantly to the permission of his knees and leapt forward into a gallop. Sand flew up under its hooves. His keffiyeh and his white robe streamed out behind and his white-clad legs blended with the horse's back as if they were one creature.

They pounded along the beach together, horse and man, spattering sparkling water that caught the bright sun so that they seemed to spread diamonds in their train.

She must have felt the thunder under her back but, as if too exhausted to react, still lay without moving. Then he was almost upon her. He pulled the horse to a standstill as she turned her head against the sand to look up.

Her eyes found his face. Her mouth fell open in complete shock. She leapt to a sitting position, all trace of exhaustion gone. Totally disoriented, she cried, ''What are *you* doing here?''

He smiled grimly, one eyebrow raised. ''This is my land,'' he informed her.

''Your land?'' she repeated in blank amazement.

''I told you you would come to me in the end,'' he said.

\* \* \*

"What the devil's going on?" demanded Masoud al Badi, of no one in particular. "Where did that white horse come from? Where's the black horse? What the hell is Adnan doing?"

The assistant looked up from the shooting script and shrugged expressively. "I went over the scene with him, and he was on the black horse then."

The director turned his eyes back to the couple on the beach. "Isn't that Adnan out there with her? Who the hell is it? Where's Adnan?"

"I'm here," said a sheepish voice as a man in the same white desert garb as the rider came out of a nearby trailer. "It's Jafar al Hamzeh." He shrugged helplessly. "Sorry, Mr. al Badi, he said—"

*"Jaf?"* exploded the director incredulously, whirling to stare again. "Is he crazy?"

As he watched, the distant female figure struggled to her feet and started running wildly along the beach. Her naked feet left small, perfect white imprints in the wet sand as she ran.

*"Allah,* he's panicked her! She'll break her ankle!" the director cried.

A buzz ran through the set at the sound of the name, and the crew was suddenly alert. Wardrobe people and makeup artists and gofers appeared at the doors of different trailers as if someone had waved a magic wand. Jafar al Hamzeh, Cup Companion to Prince Karim, was not only rich and as handsome as the devil, he was also, at the moment, the tabloids' favourite playboy.

Things got interesting when Jafar al Hamzeh was around. If he had taken an interest in the film's star...this could be quite an adventurous shoot.

Down on the beach, the rider remained still, seated

negligently on the horse, one fist against his hip, the other casually gripping the reins, in a posture so purely, physically arrogant it was like watching a hawk or a big cat. Letting his prey run a little, his attitude said, for the sake of better sport.

The director stood as if tied, staring, while the tiny green-clad figure raced wildly down the beach. He lifted his bullhorn and shouted, but they were too far away. His voice would be feeble against the surf.

He turned and glanced around him for inspiration. Catching sight of the actor in the white desert robes, he gestured imperatively. ''Adnan, get on your horse and—''

''Oh, my God!'' someone gasped, and Masoud al Badi turned again.

The rider had spurred his horse to action at last. The white beast responded eagerly, leaping forward to the chase, and within moments was close behind the running woman. He did not slacken speed.

The director cursed helplessly into the bullhorn.

''Jaf! God damn it, *Jaf!*''

Those watching gave a collective gasp as, in the distance, the horseman now dropped the reins against the horse's neck. Like a trick rider in the circus, he leaned sideways out of the saddle, clinging with his knees, while the horse, galloping perilously close to the fleeing woman, moved abreast of her.

''Is he trying to run her down?'' Masoud demanded furiously.

She screamed something, turning to flail her arms at him, but to no avail. The horseman's hands caught her firmly around her slim waist and he lifted her effortlessly as he straightened in the saddle. Suddenly she was sitting in front of him on the horse, being held tight in one ruthless arm. With the other he captured the reins again and urged the horse forward.

"Put me down!" Lisbet shouted wildly. "Are you trying to kill me? What the hell do you think you're doing?"

"But you dared me, Lisbet," he murmured, his face alight with a devilish smile. "When a woman dares a man of spirit it is because she wishes to provoke him to action. But she must beware. The action may not be exactly what she wished."

Lisbet gasped in outrage. "Do you imagine I wanted you to—! How did you get here, anyway? How did you know where we were?"

He smiled down into her face, showing all his teeth.

"Do you take me for a weakling, who waits for circumstance to assist him? You are not so foolish!"

Her heart was beating uncomfortably fast. At this it kicked hard. "What do you mean?"

Jaf laughed and encouraged the horse, forcing her to cling to his chest for balance. The white horse galloped effortlessly along the perfect, smooth sand with his double load. Water diamonds splashed up around them and fell back into the glittering sea.

"What do you mean, you didn't wait for circumstance?" she repeated, more loudly.

"You will learn what I mean," he said.

Once they were lovers, but that was long ago. No, not in a previous life, though such is always possible. They had met almost a year ago, when her friend and his brother were struggling through suspicion and misunderstanding towards love.

There had been no suspicion or misunderstanding

for Jaf and Lisbet. Not at the beginning. For them to look had been to love—or at least, to desire. And from desire there had been nothing to bar the rapid progress to completion.

Of a sort. But soon he came to feel that sexual completion was not all that he wanted. He had wanted, in the words of that still echoing song, to get inside her head.

She had not wanted him there. He would hold her head between his two powerful hands in the moment when passion was about to drag them away from shore and into those unfathomable depths—he would cup her head, as if it were one of the precious, paper-thin jade cups in his late father's treasury of antique art, and gaze into her eyes, watching for a sign that what swept his heart also touched her. But she would only laugh and turn her head away or, if his hands were too insistent, close her eyes as the pleasure his body made for her coursed through her.

When he became demanding, she had warned him. "Don't dream about me, Jaf. Don't look at me and see the mother of your babies. That's not who I am."

It drove him wild. Of course when he looked at her he saw the mother of his sons and daughters. He saw the grandmother of his grandchildren.

"Come with me to Barakat when I go," he pleaded, for soon he would have to return. "A visit. See whether you could live there. We would live there for part of the year only. It's a beautiful country, Lisbet."

She had smiled in that way that infuriated him—remote and untouchable. "I'm sure it is. Anna loves it there." Anna was her friend, who had married his brother—once love had conquered, as it must. "Maybe I'd love the country, too. But that's not the point, is it? It's not about Barakat versus England. It's about marriage versus freedom. And I did warn you, Jaf. Right at the start.''

''Freedom!'' he had exclaimed impatiently. How could she be so blind? ''What freedom? The freedom to grow old alone? To be without children to comfort you?''

A look he did not understand had crossed over her face then, and her eyes became shuttered. ''Exactly,'' she said cheerfully, her voice belying the expression on her face. ''The freedom to grow old alone, without children to comfort me. We're mismatched, Jaf. If you would just face that simple—''

His hand urgently clasped her neck to stop the words in her throat. ''We are not mismatched,'' he growled. ''We are the perfect mating that others only dream of.''

She had the grace to blush. ''I didn't mean sex.''

He stared at her, shaking his head, until her gaze fell. Then he said gently, to the top of her bent head. ''Sex is only one of the ways in which we are matched, Lisbet. Do you think I do not know how you struggle to hide from me? Do you understand that what I am saying means that such hiding is unnecessary?''

She had looked at him then, smiling defiantly. ''You're imagining things, Jaf.''

But he knew that he was not.

# Two

Lisbet kicked her heels futilely at the horse's powerful, rhythmically flexing shoulders. She was sitting side-saddle in front of Jaf, one hip tilted against the low pommel. In spite of his imprisoning arm, it felt precarious, and she was forced to cling to him for stability.

"Where do you think you're taking me?" she cried.

"My home is a few miles away," Jaf told her.

Lisbet gasped. "Your home! Are you crazy? Take me back to t—"

His dark eyes met hers with hard anger. "Do not speak to me in this tone, Lisbet."

She quailed, then forced her courage up. "I'm in the middle of shooting a film, Jaf!" she cried. "You've already wrecked a scene we were hoping to get in the can in one take! Take me back to the set!"

"When I am through with you," Jaf agreed, his

voice grating against her already electrified nerve ends.

Her blood surged up under her skin at the pressure of his unforgiving hold against her waist. Her body told her it had been long, too long. But she wasn't going to admit her weakness to him.

"When you're—how *dare* you? What are you planning, Jaf? Rape? Let me go!"

He laughed. "Do you pretend that rape would be possible between us? How long has it been, Lisbet? Have you counted the days?"

"No, I have not!"

"The weeks?"

"Stop this horse!"

She reached for the reins, one hand still of necessity clinging to his chest, but he simply knocked her hand aside.

"The months?" he prodded. "I want to know, Lisbet."

"It's over six months!" she snapped. "And I was not coun—"

"How much over six months?" he demanded relentlessly.

"I have no idea!"

"How much?"

"It's seven months and three weeks, damn you!"

"And how many days?"

"How the hell am I supposed to know?"

"You know."

"I do not know!"

"Then I will tell you. Four days. It is seven months, three weeks and four days since you told me to do my worst, Lisbet. Did no instinct warn you that it might be dangerous to come to my country so soon?"

"You call nearly eight months *soon?*" she gibed. "I thought you'd have forgotten my name by now."

"You were disappointed that I did not come after you?" he inquired softly. "Ah, Lisbet, if I had known..."

She stiffened, feeling the silky edges of the trap he had laid for her.

"No, I was not! After all your ranting, I was relieved."

"Liar!"

"Don't speak to me in that tone of voice, Jaf!" she snapped furiously.

He laughed. "Ah, my fire spitter! I had almost forgotten the delights of tangling with you. But we will have the pleasure of learning them all again."

"Spitfire," she said coldly. "If you're going to insult me, at least get your English right."

"Spitfire?" he repeated. "Isn't the Spitfire an aeroplane?"

"A fighter plane," she told him sweetly. "And as for the delights of warfare with me, the little Spitfire defeated the Luftwaffe, so don't get your hopes up."

He raised surprised eyebrows. "You call this war?"

"What would you call it?"

He shook his head, and she felt the muscles of his arm bunch as he drew on the horse's reins. The horse slowed.

Ahead of them a high ridge of rock erupting from the sand stretched into the sea, barring their path—one of the isolated fingers of the distant mountain range that brooded over the scene, as if, in this desperately hot, inhospitable climate, even the mountains yearned and reached for the sea.

He drew the horse to a walk, and they entered the

shadow of the ridge with relief. Lisbet put both her hands above his on the reins and now he allowed her to pull the horse to a standstill.

"One way or another, I'm going back to the set," she announced.

His jaw clenched with the possessive ferocity that had made her run the first time. "Not one hour to spare for your ex-lover?"

"While I'm working? I'm a professional, Jaf," she said. "Don't expect me to fall in with your amateur, playboy attitude to life."

His eyes glinted with an indecipherable expression. "Ah," he said. "So you didn't forget me entirely."

"It was a little difficult to forget you entirely!" she snapped. "You're in the tabloids every week."

"One of the benefits of fame I hadn't foreseen," he observed blandly.

Now he believed she had been following his career in the papers, she realized with irritation. It would have been better to pretend she knew nothing of his new status as the tabloids' favourite bad boy.

But she couldn't stop herself complaining, "That's a heady lifestyle you've got yourself. I was particularly entranced by the gold-plated limousine."

He shrugged disparagingly. "Par for the course in these parts."

"Nice for some. But I have a job to do."

Her hands on the reins, she guided the horse into a 180-degree turn. Jaf allowed it, but when she tried to spur the horse to move, it froze into immobility.

She was startled to see how far they had come. She had expected to see, in the distance, the cluster of trailers, equipment, umbrellas and people that marked the filming location, but the sand was empty. They were alone. A thrill of fear shivered through her. In this barren landscape and merciless, unforgiving climate, she was at his mercy.

Just what she had always feared.

"Damn it!" Lisbet exclaimed, urging the reins, and nudging the horse's foreleg with her bare heels. The horse might as well have been carved of wood. "Move damn it!" she cried. And then, "What have you done to this horse?"

He laughed, showing white teeth. His eyes sparkled in a way she remembered they had even in London's damp. Here in the harsh sunshine the look dazzled her.

"Firouz and I have been together for six years," he said. "If you understood me as well as he does…"

Lisbet gritted her teeth. "It would be better if *you* understood *me!*" she snapped. "Now, are you going to get this horse to move and take me back to the set, or am I going to get down and walk?"

It was a long way in such heat, and if she did not get lost, she would get sunburn, if not actual sunstroke. She could feel the prickle of drying salt on her skin and knew that the sea had washed off some, if not all, of her protection.

"You can't walk in the sun," he told her, looking down at her bare legs, the rise of her breasts in the revealing neckline of the costume. It was a look she remembered all too well. Her skin tingled under the drying salt. "You are nearly naked. My house is cool inside. It is among trees, a date plantation."

"Take me back," she said stonily, kicking futilely at the immovable horse. Her eyes scoured the horizon for some sign that someone was coming to her rescue. "They must have called the police by now. They must think you're a kidnapper."

"But that is what I am," Jaf pointed out.

"What have you done to Adnan?" she almost shrieked.

"Your imagination is very vivid, but perhaps that is a professional necessity for an actress," he said. Lisbet ground her teeth. She had never had an easy time controlling her temper around him. "I have done nothing to Adnan Amani except ease his financial worries for the immediate future."

"You *bribed* him to let you take his place?" she cried, outraged.

"Would you prefer that I had knocked him on the head and tied him up? Violence should always be a last resort," he chided.

"Of course I wouldn't prefer—" Lisbet began heatedly, then realized that he was succeeding in putting her in the wrong. She heaved a breath.

"Take me back to the set."

"On one condition."

"To hell with your condition!"

"You must have dinner with me this evening."

"Dinner! If that was all you wanted, why didn't you come to Gazi and Anna's? You must know I've been staying there!"

Coming to the Barakat Emirates to shoot the movie a week ago, she had naturally stayed with Anna and Gazi. It would have been natural for Jaf to visit them, but he made no move to try and see her. "We usually see him once or twice a week," Anna had said apologetically. "He must be very busy."

Lisbet had been half relieved, half anxious. If there was going to be a meeting, she wanted to get it over with. If not, she'd have liked to be certain of that.

He laughed. "Did you miss me?"

"I never expected you to come. Why would you want to see me? Why do you now?"

"What I have to say to you is not for public consumption," he said.

Her heart pounded. She was afraid of him in this steely mood. She remembered how hard it had been to shut him out of her life. It had taken all her determination. "I'm not interested," she said stonily.

"You do not agree to come?"

"We finished months ago, Jaf. It's over and it's going to stay that way."

He seemed to make no move, and yet the horse lifted a delicate foreleg and stepped around in place, till it was facing the rocky ridge and the sea again.

"My house is beyond this point," he said. The horse moved into the sea. "It is well protected. Once we are there, no one will reach you except with my permission."

"Let me down!" she cried.

She struggled, but he held her tight, and the horse moved faster. She could not risk jumping, especially when she couldn't be sure of the surface under the water. If her foot landed on a rock, if she fell or the horse kicked her...

"Now, or tonight, Lisbet? One way or another, you will see me." The horse was moving into deeper water, on a heading around the thrusting finger of rock.

She could feel determination in him. Her feet were now brushing the surface of the water. Her body skittered with nervous anticipation.

After the months of silence, she had begun to believe that he had forgotten her, forgotten all his protestations of love. During the past week of waiting every night on tenterhooks for him to turn up at dinner, she had been convinced. And now, suddenly, here he was, angry, unforgiving, punitive.

She felt disoriented. She suddenly felt she didn't know him. He was in his own country, on his own territory, taking her she knew not where. She was a foreigner, and he was influential here.

"All right!" she exploded, furious at her own capitulation.

The horse stopped instantly. Jaf frowned into her eyes. "You will have dinner with me tonight?"

"Yes, I'll have dinner with you, damn you! But not at your house. I'll go with you to a restaurant, and that's final. So if you were expecting more than dinner, forget it! A face over a meal is all you'll get."

His head inclined with regal acceptance, making her feel like a rude peasant in the presence of the lord of the manor. "But of course," Jaf said, as if she had made an indelicate remark. "What else?"

Firouz turned in place and began to pace back out of the water, as precise as a circus horse.

"Just as long as you realize there'll be no sex for dessert," Lisbet said defiantly.

"Do *you* realize it?" Jaf said.

They met two dune buggies halfway. Jaf laughed and reined in. "Your rescuers are only a little late," he said.

"Lisbet, are you all right?" the director demanded, piling out of one of the vehicles in half-crazed concern. "Is everything okay?"

They had galloped in silence, Jaf's chest against her back, the horse moving powerfully under her thighs, in a twin reminder of masculine might. Lisbet was filled with such a churning of conflicting and varied emotions she couldn't find words.

One of the grips was there to help her down, but the dark, stocky director pushed him aside and solicitously reached up for her himself. She slipped out of Jaf's strong hold and down onto the sand, and only when his protection was gone felt the loss.

Jaf's face was stone as he watched the movement drag the dress of her skirt up around her hips, revealing the full length of her legs and the lacy underwear.

Masoud, glancing up at Jaf, let her go a moment too quickly. Lisbet staggered a little and then straightened.

"No, everything is not all right," she informed the director in quiet fury. "Do you know this man? I won't work while he's on the set," she said, storming off towards the dune buggy.

She was hoping for an argument, because Jaf was certain to lose. But she might have known better. She had taken no more than two steps when there came the sound of hooves. Involuntarily, Lisbet turned. Jafar al Hamzeh, his robes flying, magnificent on the white horse, was riding back the way they had come.

Minutes later, Lisbet slammed into the welcome if erratic air conditioning of her trailer. Tina, her dresser, wide-eyed with unspoken curiosity, fluttered in anxious concern while she struggled with the buttons on her costume.

"You've been in the sun too long! Is your nose burned? I *told* Masoud, less than half an hour and then we need to reapply the sun block!"

Lisbet was suddenly exhausted. Her meeting with Jaf seemed to have drained her of energy. "Save it, Tina. I want a shower," she said, stripping off the torn costume.

Then she was under the cooling spray. Cast and crew had all been asked to use the fresh water sparingly, since it had to be trucked onto the site, but Lisbet forgot that as she held her face to the cool stream.

If only other things could be so easily forgotten.

She had met Jafar al Hamzeh when he came to ask for her help. Her best friend, Anna Lamb, was in trouble and needed her. Naturally, she had agreed to go with him.

There was an immediate spark between them. He made no secret of his attraction to her. That evening, having given Anna the help she needed, Lisbet had had to leave for work—shooting an exterior scene for an episode of a television series, on Hampstead Heath. Jaf had driven her to the location and then stayed to keep her company—all night.

She would never forget the electricity of that night. Sitting in the deeper dark behind the floodlights, bundled up against the chill, she and Jaf gazed into each other's eyes, talking about nothing and everything, while she waited to be called. Each time she went on set to do a take, she feared he would have gone when she got back, but he was always there, waiting.

There was a connection between them like a taut, singing wire, and over the course of that long night, the electric charge got stronger and stronger till Jaf was more blinding than the floodlights.

He had taken her home in the limousine, and she had invited him in for coffee. As they entered the darkened apartment he kissed her, suddenly, hungrily, as if he had let go a self-restraint of banded steel. It was their first kiss, and it exploded on their lips with fiery sweetness. The thought of it, even now, could make chills run over her skin.

She would never forget that first time, making love with Jaf as the sun came up over the damp roofs of London. Not if she lived to be a hundred.

Afterwards, she had worried that, coming from so different a culture, he would think her cheap, despise her for such ease of conquest. He left her with a passionate kiss in the morning, saying he would call her soon, and her fear whispered that for him it had been no more than a one-night stand.

The limousine was waiting for her at the curb when she left the television studio that evening. Her heart leapt so hard she staggered. It took her—or perhaps, she had told herself, giggling, in the lush, leather-lined splendour of the Rolls, *swept* was the more appropriate word—to the Dorchester Hotel.

No one at the Dorchester even raised an eyebrow at her grubby sweatpants, the frayed sweater, the ragged bomber jacket, her shiny, just-scrubbed face, the hair caught up with a couple of jumbo clips, the extra-long scarf taking three turns around her neck.

"You might have given a girl some warning!" she protested, when Jaf opened the door on the penthouse suite. He was standing in an entrance hall bigger than her whole flat.

His smile made her drunker than champagne. "What should I have warned you about?"

He put out a hand and drew her inside, and before she could begin to answer his mouth closed on hers, hungry and demanding.

Later, they lay lazily entwined in each other, while he stroked her back, her hip, her thigh. Above them, a huge skylight showed them the stars. His hold was light, and yet he seemed to protect and enclose her. She had never felt so safe.

They looked up at the stars, and he complained at how pale they were, compared to the sky in Barakat.

"Once, when I was very young," Jaf murmured, "I was with my grandfather as he examined a collection of diamonds. I can still see those stones dropping onto the black velvet cushion my grandfather had set down. They sparkled with black fire. They dazzled my eyes."

"Mmmm," she said, as his hand painted little sparkles of electricity along her spine.

"My mother said afterwards, though I don't remember that part of it, that I absolutely insisted on touching them. All I remember is that I was lifted up and put my hands out, and my grandfather dropped diamonds onto my palms. It was a moment that thrilled me beyond description."

Lisbet smiled, picturing him as a little boy, trembling with delight. "I wonder why it had such impact."

"Because I thought I was touching the stars, Lisbet," he said softly. "That is what the stars are like in my country. They are diamonds. I really believed that my grandfather had brought down stars and a piece of sky. It was a moment of almost mystical ecstasy."

Lisbet smiled, touched and charmed by the image. She turned her head and looked up at the night sky. "Yes, I see."

Jaf's arms tightened around her. He gazed down into her upturned face and saw starlight in her eyes. For a moment there was pure silence.

"I have never had such a feeling again until now," he whispered, lifting one hand to her cheek. "Till now I never touched the stars again."

# Three

――――

"**H**e's here," Lisbet's dresser said breathlessly, tapping and entering the trailer that was Lisbet's living quarters for the duration of the location shoot. Tina was trying to disguise her excitement, but still her tone of voice irritated Lisbet.

"You sound like a pensioner meeting the Queen," she muttered.

"Funny you should say that. When I was twelve I met Princess Diana. It was the most exciting moment of my life," Tina said with a grin. "I've met plenty of celebrities since then, but in this business the glitter goes fast. Nothing's ever had quite the impact. Until now."

Lisbet knew she was joking, but couldn't help responding in a repressive tone, "What's so hot about Jafar al Hamzeh?"

"Hey, you're the one who's going to have dinner with him!"

Lisbet shrugged. No one here was aware that she had known Jaf before, and she had no intention of letting them know.

Tina gave her a look. "You do know he's one of Prince Karim's Cup Companions, don't you?"

"Yes, I know."

But Tina was in full swing. "So's his brother Gazi. In these parts that's sort of like being a rock star, except that they also have political clout. Rashid—one of the grips—told me that the tradition of the Cup Companions goes back a very long way, to pre-Islamic times, but in the old days they were just the guys the king relaxed with. They were deliberately excluded from the executive process. Nowadays, they form what amounts to the prince's cabinet. Most of them have specific responsibilities, and they all have a lot of influence, right across the board. And they're as loyal as it gets, to each other and the princes."

Lisbet wanted to shout at her to shut up. But she concentrated on her lipstick and did not answer.

"He's rich, too, Lisbet—stinking rich, since his father died, according to the scuttlebutt on the set—and, they say, very generous. Also spending mad. Those stories in the press aren't all scandalmongering, apparently. He's going through his inheritance like water over a falls. He dropped half a million barakatis in one sitting at the casino a couple of nights ago, and got up completely unfazed. If you play it right, you could dip your bucket into the flow and put something away for a comfortable old age."

She paused, but Lisbet was still carefully outlining

her lips in a pinky beige. Tina frowned. With that outfit, her lips should be wine-red.

"And incredibly sexy, on top of it. What about the way he galloped after you on the beach—woo! We were all practically fainting. And when he actually picked you up on the fly—I swear I got sensory burn from here. What did he say when he had you on the horse?"

"Nothing much." Lisbet set down the lipstick brush and sat back to examine the result. "Certainly I don't recall hearing any apology for risking my life in a circus stunt."

Tina manifestly disbelieved her indifference. She waggled her eyebrows.

"Well, anytime he wants to perform a stunt with me, he's welcome!" Tina said. "Did you know he was on the Barakat Emirates' Olympic equestrian team in 1996, and they got a gold? And in his wild youth, when he was at university in the States, he spent his holidays in a circus or rodeo or something."

Lisbet knew it all, but she wasn't going to have everyone on the set raking over her ancient affair with Jaf if she could help it.

"A rodeo would be just the place for him. The wonder is why he ever left," she said. She got to her feet and checked herself in the mirror. She was wearing a knee-length tunic top over pants, all in a soft knitted oatmeal silk, a few shades darker than her hair.

"You've got to be joking!" The dresser was unstoppable now. "The man oozes sensuality. He reminds me of those old French movie stars. Belmondo. Delon. *Je t'aime, moi non plus.* Ooooh." Tina picked up the matching calf-length silk coat and held it as

Lisbet slipped her arms into the sleeves. "I wish it were me he was after. Yum!"

"He is not after me!" Lisbet said irritably. She shrugged into the coat and reached for her evening bag. Tina's litany was only making her more nervous. She wondered why she had capitulated to his ridiculous ultimatum. She should have realized he couldn't make it stick.

Maybe she just couldn't resist seeing him one more time.

"Silly me, I thought he was," Tina corrected herself in a tone of extreme irony. "He was just warning you off his land, then, was he? Did you know he owns the whole stretch of beach along here?" she added in parentheses. "We're on his land."

Lisbet concentrated on her reflection. Her leather sandals and handbag matched the oatmeal silk, and her long hair was held back with a tiny braided ribbon of the same colour. She had chosen the outfit carefully, for its cool, undramatic elegance. It was the furthest thing from deliberately sexy, she told herself, that you could find.

Her earrings were thin squares of beaten gold. With them she wore a gold chain necklace...and on the third finger of her left hand, a large pearl ring.

"You look fabulous!" Tina said, hoping her tone disguised her faint disappointment. She began unnecessarily brushing Lisbet down, and tweaked a fold of her coat. She wished Lisbet had left her hair loose or worn a touch of colour. Anyone would think she was deliberately dressing her warm sexuality down, but Tina couldn't believe anyone would act in such a stupid and self-defeating way.

It must be nerves. Because Lisbet, as her dresser had quickly learned, had a craftsman's eye for what suited her. She could always add just that personal touch to a costume that made it her own, giving it a flair the camera loved. That was Tina's yardstick for what made a star.

But as the actress moved to the door Tina blinked and took a second look. Maybe Lisbet knew what she was doing after all. She supposed Arabs were as susceptible to the Ice Maiden myth as other men, and the hinting motion of Lisbet's body under that silk might just drive a guy wild.

At first she had given herself up to the passion that consumed them.

They had a devastating, emotionally tormenting, crazily passionate time together. Like nothing she had ever experienced. Sometimes she felt drunk, so drunk she was reeling. Sometimes she felt that Jaf had her heart in his hand. A word, a look, had a power over her that was completely outside her previous experience.

It frightened her. Not just his possessiveness, but her own response to it. And she had plenty of reason to fear having her life taken over.

It touched Lisbet on an old but ever tender wound.

It had been out of motives of love that her father had deliberately got her mother pregnant, in order to put an end to her promised stage career and keep her with him.

That had been a long time ago, when the morality of the swinging sixties hadn't quite reached the small Welsh mining village where the young lovers lived.

Gillian Raine had won a place at drama school and was waiting for the summer to end before leaving for London and another life. Her lover, Edward MacArthur, had already done what every man in the village did—he had started work down the coal mines.

The cautionary tale of her mother's murdered dreams had been burned into Lisbet from a child. How he had pleaded with her to stay home and marry him. How she had had to give in when she learned she was pregnant… *Never give up your dreams, girls,* her mother had warned them.

As they grew into teenagers, the story became clearer. Then Gillian told her daughters how that life-changing pregnancy had occurred. Told them of the fateful night when Edward had asked her to turn her back on drama college, stay at home and marry him….

Gillian had resisted all Edward's pleading and, when he knew he had lost the argument, he began to kiss her.

Her daughters, educated in the new model of the world, had asked breathlessly, "Did Dad date rape you, Mama?"

She had laughed impatiently. "No, no, don't you see what I'm trying to tell you? He was such a lover, your father, he just—girls, he just kissed me till…" She sighed. "Always before we'd used protection. That night he had none. But he was so passionate. I forgot everything, I wanted him and I didn't care. A few weeks later I cared, right enough. When I told him I was pregnant I saw that he'd meant to do it."

She had given up her dreams, married her lover, settled down to the grind of life as a miner's wife and produced a string of children.

And never ceased to regret the life she might have had.

Lisbet had listened closely to the terrible warnings. She didn't want a life like her mother's. Always regretting what she hadn't done. *If it hadn't been for you lot, that would be me up there,* she would say when they sat around the television watching the latest costume drama.

Still, life had been more or less happy before the closure of the mines. Until then her father had come home at night exhausted and black with coal dust, maybe, but he was a man who held up his head. A man who made his wife smile with secret anticipation over the dinner table when he gave her burning looks out of those dark Celtic eyes.

Lisbet was just approaching her teens when the great miners' strike was called, the prime minister infamously sent in the mounted strikebreakers, and an era came to an end. When the dust and blood cleared, the coal mines were finished, and so was Lisbet's father.

More than his mine was gone, more than his job. His faith in British justice and fair play, and much else besides, was destroyed. His vision of himself had been shattered.

He had never worked again, except for casual labour here and there. It was his wife who went to work now, an even deeper shame for a man like him. Gillian worked in the little fish and chip shop, practically the only enterprise that survived the economic disaster that had engulfed the village, and came home smelling of cigarette smoke and half-rancid cooking fat, her hair lank and her once-beautiful face shiny with grease.

Her husband had hated the fact that his wife now had to work, without having the will to get up and change his life. He was a failure in the first source of pride he had, and it unmanned him completely. He began to drink.

The only bright side had been that there were no mines now for Lisbet's brothers to go down. Their choice was different—join the ranks of the unemployed, or leave their village.

The MacArthurs were all bright. They had all gone on to higher education, in those days when, thank God, students from poor backgrounds were still being given full study grants. They had all worked hard, done well, gone on to good jobs.

Lisbet was always the special one. Lisbet, inheriting her mother's beauty as well as her taste for theatre, had gone to a prestigious London drama college, with the weight of both their dreams on her shoulders. There she had left behind her musical regional accent and her father's name. She chose her mother's maiden name as a stage name, and Elizabeth Raine MacArthur became Lisbet Raine.

At graduation, she had won the most coveted prize, the Olivier Medal. Since then, she had worked steadily, mostly in television, getting bigger and better parts as time went by.

Lisbet knew at first hand that real security lay only in oneself. Not in marriage or a man. Not in letting someone else run your life according to their own tastes. The only real security was to become someone on your own merits. Only achievement lasted. Her mother was living proof that in the end you could count on no one but yourself.

For a woman, love was full of pitfalls. So, very soon after her affair with Jaf began, Lisbet was thinking of her independence. She didn't want any misunderstandings about her expectations—or Jaf's.

He bought her jewellery for her birthday, a beautiful gold bangle studded with rubies and diamonds. She was thrilled, but said with a smile, "It'll come in handy to pawn next time I'm between jobs." And she laughed when he furiously said that of course she would apply to him if she were ever broke, all the rest of her life.

"Oh, sure. And how will I get to you through your staff and what will I say when your secretary says you don't know the name and can I tell him what it's about?"

"I will forget nothing about you," Jaf said, kissing her with ruthless passion. "From the first moment I saw you, there is not a moment I will forget."

She thought he was the most wonderful, thoughtful lover a woman could have. But that only increased her risk. "Your lies are liquid honey," she told him softly. "So sweet, so delicious."

"You don't believe it because you don't *want* to believe it," he had railed at her. "You avoid commitment by pretending to think that I am not serious, Lisbet. You tell yourself it is impossible for a rich and influential man to love you and you ignore the fact that your friend and my brother have married!"

On one level, it was true. When Anna and Gazi married, it shook her badly. Marriage was not for her, and she had been deeply dismayed by the yearnings that had surfaced as she stood beside her friend during the sweetly moving wedding service.

Maybe that was the first moment she understood that her affair with Jaf was a very dangerous liaison, and would have to end.

When Lisbet opened the door of her trailer, the first thing she saw, a few yards away down one of the metal roads that were temporarily crisscrossing the desert sand, was a Rolls. The chauffeur, in polo shirt and trousers, was wiping down the immaculate paintwork while chewing industriously on a toothpick. The limousine was a spotless, creamy white. The bumpers and handles—all the trim that should be chrome—were gold.

So it was true. She hadn't believed it, reading about the car in the papers. It was a long way from the Jaf she had known.

But maybe he'd just known that a thing like the gold-plated Rolls wouldn't go over very well in laid-back Britain.

A large number of the crew seemed to be lounging in doorways and under awnings, with no apparent purpose. Lisbet frowned and shook her head in disbelief as she realized that they were actually hanging around to watch the meeting between her and Jaf.

This afternoon's little drama had ignited people's imaginations.

The director, Masoud, was standing by his office trailer, talking to someone. The other man stood with his back to her in a black kaftan and keffiyah. It was the kind of dress worn, at times, by every male from waiter to prince in the Barakat Emirates.

Lisbet paused for a moment in the doorway, gazing at him. She had never seen Jafar al Hamzeh in Eastern clothing before, unless you counted this afternoon's Lawrence of Arabia getup, but she knew it was him.

He seemed to have sensors on his back, too, because he instantly straightened and turned around and stared along the tiny ''street'' to the door of her trailer.

Jaf stood motionless, just looking, as she stepped out of her trailer and moved towards him. Her hair was drawn back to reveal the soft curves of her cheek and throat, the delicate sculpting of her ears, where beaten gold glowed in the late-afternoon sunlight. Flowing silk just darker than her hair brushed her body with every movement, simultaneously revealing and cloaking the curve of arm, thigh, breast. Blood rushed to his hands, burning him with the sensual memory of those curves.

Lisbet, under the intensity of his gaze, half stumbled, her fingers automatically spreading to steady herself. Jaf came to meet her, while the chauffeur stowed his polishing cloth and opened the door of the sumptuously appointed, gold-plated limousine. He was still resolutely chewing the toothpick.

The elegant Rolls-Royce emblem had been removed from the nose of the car, and Lisbet's eyes were irresistibly drawn to the grotesque gold statuette that took its place—a full-breasted, naked woman in a kind of swan dive, her back arched and her hair streaming out behind her.

Well, she had seen a picture of it, but she hadn't believed it.

''And some people say Arabs have no taste!'' she marvelled.

''Out here this counts as the stripped-down model,'' Jaf assured her.

"So I see." She bent forward to peer inside the car. It was a vision of luscious white leather, burnished wood, Persian carpets, and more gold trim.

"What a lot of buttons!" she exclaimed in mock wonder, catching sight of a large panel of gold-plated switches on the armrest. "What do they all do?"

"I can only say it would be inadvisable to push any without prior notice."

She couldn't help laughing at that, but Jaf's mouth suddenly lost its smile. He gazed at her with an unreadable expression that held no humour.

"Get in," he said.

Sudden, superstitious fear pulsed in her. She'd never seen this side of him. She'd never seen him dressed like this. Here in his own country—on his own property—he was a stranger to her. A man who owned a gold-plated car.

She didn't have a clue what he wanted from her tonight. But he looked as if he meant to get it.

She stood helplessly at the car door, battling with herself. She half felt she should refuse to go with this stranger, but her heart was beating with excitement and anticipation as well as nervous fear. His presence still affected her physically. Probably it always would.

He didn't repeat his command, giving her nothing to kick against. The chauffeur was standing there expectantly, and everyone was more or less discreetly watching. Mostly less. After a moment Lisbet obediently bent and got in.

For all the ostentation, the leather seat was silky smooth, divinely comfortable. She slipped over to the right side as Jaf followed her inside and the door closed after him.

Masoud, the director, lifted his hand in farewell, and members of the crew stared unabashedly now as the car backed and turned, and carefully started along the metal slats of the temporary road.

They had scarcely moved beyond the immediate area of the movie camp, where desert stretched all around them, when Jaf reached out to grasp her wrist. Lisbet's breath hissed with surprise.

"What is this?" he asked softly, lifting her hand. Left hand. His voice was deep, and running with dangerous undercurrents. Like the sea.

"You can see for yourself, a pearl solitaire with diamond chips."

He gave one slow blink, silently watching her. It was totally unnerving.

The sun was setting over the water. It had taken on a rich glow, painting the sea with thick gold. On the other side of the sky, behind the mountains, darkness approached. A portent, maybe.

Jaf remained silent, his eyes burning into hers. In spite of herself she was compelled to speak.

"An engagement ring, Jaf," she said, a little more loudly than necessary.

He didn't move, but now she was nervous of him. His eyes darkened all at once, in a way she knew.

He touched a switch, and the window beside him rolled smoothly down. The fine sand dust caused by their passing swirled gently into the car.

Lisbet gazed at him in puzzlement, blinking as his grip tightened on her wrist. Then he lifted her hand, dragged the ring down the length of her finger, and flung it out the window.

He didn't speak a word. His hand dropped to the panel and the window glided silently up again.

Lisbet's heart seemed to stop. Whorls of furious excitement exploded into a dance over her skin. "How *dare* you?" she choked.

He gave a contemptuous flick of his chin in the direction of the vanished ring. "It wasn't even genuine. Is the man a fool? Are you?"

Lisbet bit her lip. She had borrowed it from the costume mistress's collection only an hour ago. She'd thought it looked pretty good, but she ought to have known that Jaf would know the difference at a glance.

"I know it's not real!" she improvised wildly. "We're both stretched financially at the moment, but he said he wasn't having me coming out here to sheikh country without some badge of possession on my finger."

Jaf stared at her, so bemused she almost laughed. She was doing her best on the spur of the moment, but she had to agree, it was a pretty feeble story.

"And who is this fool who expects a cheap *souk* ring to be enough to hold his claim to a woman like you?"

"His name is Roger," Lisbet said furiously.

"Roger what?"

She gave him a look, her lips firmly closed. He released her hand at last, and she pulled it back to her lap. It was pins and needles up to her elbow, as though his touch had cut off the blood supply, which was ridiculous.

"Six months ago you were not the marrying kind," he reminded her harshly.

"People change."

He was stretched against the upholstery, one arm along the back of the seat, the other elbow propped against the armrest, but she didn't make the mistake of thinking he was relaxed. His tension shimmered in the air.

"And how have you changed, Lisbet?"

The ring had been the impulse of the moment, like putting on a magic talisman to avert the evil eye. She should have known he wouldn't let it pass without question.

But she wasn't exactly rehearsed in the role of adoring fiancée.

"Could we change the subject, please?"

"You don't like to talk about him?"

"Not to you."

"Does Roger understand that he is marrying a woman with no heart?" His anger was being ruthlessly kept in check. "Does he give up the desire for children for the sake of possessing you?"

The Rolls was still creeping along the steel road. There was no other way to travel along such a surface, but Lisbet's claustrophobia was intensified by the dead slow pace. Long purple-grey shadows stretched out from the dunes over the rippling surface of the sand.

"Roger and I are perfectly agreed on what we want from the future, thank you!"

He smiled, but it was the smile of a tiger. "Poor Lisbet."

"What does *that* mean?"

"You will never be happy with a yes-man."

"Roger is not a yes-man!"

"Then he is a fool. A man who does not want children is a fool, or a liar."

She thought of her father, and her heart hardened. "All men aren't as primitive as you, Jaf."

His eyes flashed dangerously. "Be careful. You might make me imagine that you are speaking from your desires rather than your observations."

"Is that a threat?" she demanded shrilly.

His hand moved and his fingers caught the errant little curl of hair at her temple that could never be tamed. He stroked it around his forefinger while little jolts of electricity rushed down her temple and jaw and shot into her body.

"I only say what you should already know."

Lisbet gritted her teeth. What a fool she had been to come out with him thinking to find protection in a cheap ring! She slapped his hand away.

"I think you're confusing me with someone else."

"I could prove to you that I am not."

"No, you could not!" Lisbet said quickly.

"Too loyal to Roger to fan an old flame?"

"Of course!"

"Did you tell him about me?"

"Briefly, along with several others."

One eyebrow flickered.

"Does he know you're seeing me tonight?"

Lisbet hesitated for a fatal moment. "Yes," she said. She knew it sounded like a lie.

He nodded, as if to himself. "Did you plan it, then, Lisbet? You are engaged to another man, and yet you risked coming here, living at my brother's house. What did you tell yourself? That I could be put off by a ring from the bazaar and a distant fiancé?

"But no, you knew better than that!" he answered himself. "What was in your mind? Another quick, meaningless affair? Is that what you planned for when you came? A little reprise of passion with a barbarian before going back to marry a safe man, a man from your own culture? Did you hope I would be too hungry for your body to turn away from the crumbs you offer? Did you cast me in the part of the beggar at the gates, Lisbet? You mistook me.''

His lips smiled. But as his black eyes met hers a shiver of danger traced her skin. As if she were looking into a cave where a wolf lurked in the darkness.

''Do you tell yourself that I still want you, Lisbet? Do you imagine that it is impossible to kill a love such as mine?'' His voice grated over her soul, rough and sharp together. ''Or did you hope to find that I had now developed a taste for heartless passion like yours?''

The tirade was more than she could stand. With a silent cry she launched herself at him, both arms lifting, to beat him or strangle him, she hardly knew.

But Jaf was an Olympic-level sportsman, and his reflexes were well honed. His hands snapped out and caught her wrists in midair, and suddenly everything changed. His eyes darkened as he drew her close and held her wrists in an unbreakable grip.

''Do not push too hard, Lisbet,'' he warned harshly.

She could smell the scent that was uniquely Jafar, his cologne, his sweat, his skin, and it reminded her of moments of pleasure so extreme she had wept for joy.

''Let go!'' she cried.

''A woman so concerned for her freedom should be careful before she provokes a man.''

''All right, I'm sorry! Let me go!''

For answer, he dragged her wrists together and slowly, agonizingly, pulled them in against his chest, trapping them there as he wrapped his arms around her, drawing her close. Her heart leapt into her throat, choking her. A trickle of sweat moved like a tear down her temple and cheek.

"Let you go?" he repeated, in a hoarse whisper. His lips were almost brushing hers as he spoke, sending tendrils of sensation into her flesh, little harbingers of pleasure to come. "But I did let you go. If you really wanted to be free of me, Lisbet, why did you come to my country?"

# Four

**H**is mouth came down on hers, ferocious with hunger. Her heart fluttered, her blood surged. Heat like the noonday sun scorched her skin, leaving it parched and thirsty for the balm of the very touch that burned her.

His hands seemed to turn the silk of her clothes to flame, so that every twitch of her skin met more burning. His lips were unforgiving, his tongue hungry and demanding. His arms pressed and held her, imprisoning and protecting her at the same time.

Everything was contradiction, except for the central joy of hunger assuaged. That was why she couldn't move, couldn't struggle. Tell the man who has been lost in the desert not to drink. Tell the woman who was shut up in darkness not to gaze at the sun. Tell an escaped prisoner not to dance.

Jaf lifted his mouth at last and drew a shuddering breath. Released from that punishing, tormenting kiss,

Lisbet regained a little self-control. She pushed him away. She could feel tears burning her eyes without understanding what had summoned them.

"Was that supposed to be some kind of punishment?" she cried.

Jaf's eyes narrowed dangerously. "Punishment? Is that what my kiss is to you?"

Lisbet turned angrily away.

"Answer me, Lisbet! The touch of my mouth was distasteful to you?"

The lie wouldn't get past her throat.

"You think so, anyway!" she cried.

"*I* think so? What would make me think that you had changed so completely? You, the woman who melted for me as woman has never melted for man before. I hear your cries in my dreams, Lisbet, even now. And I wake to weep that you are not there. And you pretend to think that I know my touch is a punishment to you?"

She was shaking, and held her hands tightly in her lap. "I didn't say…" she began, but couldn't find any words.

He sat back into the corner, his arms spread, facing her, like a judge. His kaftan was fading into shadow now. The keffiyah stood out, circling his head. His eyes fixed on her face, locked with her gaze. In every way he seemed a stranger.

She managed to turn away, and stared out of the window. The last rays of the setting sun washed the clouds in pinky gold, and the dunes threw long navy shadows now that made the desert seem a haunted, magical place. Above, the sky was turning a deep shade that could only be called purple.

He had told her she would love the desert.

"Is that what you wanted me to believe when I received these?" he demanded, after a long, charged silence. He lifted his hands to the neckline of his robe and pulled it open, reached inside and extracted something flat and black.

Her heartbeat quickened a little, and she caught her breath as he opened the wallet and dragged a little sheaf of papers from it. With a flick of the wrist, he tossed it into her lap. The air caught it and half a dozen slips of paper showered over her.

She felt his anger like a little electric shock. Lisbet reached a shaking hand to one of the pieces of paper and drew it up, straining to see it in the gloom. Then another.

They were all identical. Personal cheques, made out to Sheikh Jafar al Hamzeh, and signed by Lisbet Raine MacArthur.

It was Jaf telling her that he wanted to set her up in a flat that was the beginning of the end.

Bit by bit, Jaf had been proving himself every bit as possessive as he was passionate. Now he wanted to own the home she lived in. If she allowed that, in a certain fundamental way she was admitting that he owned her. He would always have the upper hand.

Except for the fact that it didn't seem big enough when Jaf was there, she was comfortable in her current home. She was renting a large studio flat on the top floor of an Edwardian house in North London. It was a bit out of the city centre, but as a space it was great for the money. All her friends said so. She was lucky. She might not be so lucky another time.

If, for example, she and Jaf disagreed over something, and the only option was for her to go. She might have a hard time finding so good a place at short notice.

So she was adamant. Thanks for the thought, but she would stay where she was.

Not long after, as luck would have it, she was given her notice on the studio. The house had been unexpectedly sold to people who wanted to restore it to a single-family dwelling. And suddenly Lisbet was facing a bleak midwinter hunting for somewhere new.

She soon discovered just how lucky she had been. The rental market was at a peak, and her money wasn't going to go as far this time around. And after a dry two months on the work scene, Lisbet didn't have any money to spare.

Of course she wouldn't ask Jaf for help. By that point she had turned him down so often Jaf had given up talking about buying her a place. She regretted her decision only in weak moments.

After a couple of depressing weeks spent in fruitless apartment hunting, Lisbet realized that her best option for the moment would be to share. Eventually she found a wonderful apartment share in a breathtaking apartment with a view over Primrose Hill, an area she really loved.

For the owner it was little more than a pied-à-terre, the agent explained. A lawyer who did a lot of work in Hong Kong, she was sharing because she preferred to have someone in the flat full-time. She wanted someone responsible, someone who would take care of her plants and the beautiful furnishings and works of art.

Lisbet could scarcely believe her luck when she landed it. Sacrifices would have to be made, of course. It was more than Lisbet could comfortably afford at the moment, and her own bedroom was the smallest room in the place. But the flat itself was an absolute dream, beautifully decorated, with wonderful light and a terrace filled with plants.

Jaf was less than delighted. "How will we make love in that tiny bed?" he asked. "It is even smaller than the one in your flat. I don't see how you can be happy in such a room. You haven't even met your roommate."

"You're spoiled," she told him. "You have no idea how ordinary people live. I'd be happy in a broom cupboard in a place like that. Are you kidding? I'll have that huge place to myself at least three weeks of every month! Even if I can't stand her, for a place like that I could put up with Godzilla himself one week out of four."

So he shrugged and stopped objecting, and helped Lisbet with the move. She had to sell most of her own furniture rather than put it in storage, because she couldn't afford both storage fees and the rent, but she wasn't going to worry about that.

It wasn't till she'd been living in the place for a week that Jaf gave her the title deeds in her name.

It had all been a hoax—the Hong Kong lawyer, the sharing one week a month—it had been just a game to entice her to sell her furniture, make the move, to get her to the point of no return.

But if he was expecting trembling gratitude, his plans backfired. It had exactly the reverse effect of what he had probably designed. Maybe he had meant it for the best, but Lisbet was furious at this calculated interference in her life, casual undermining of her self-determination.

If she didn't actually feel trapped, she certainly felt

how easy it had been for him to force his will on her. And without her being at all aware of it till it was done.

Jaf couldn't see it. All he had done was circumvent a misplaced pride in her. She needed a place to live. He had provided it. What could be wrong with that? If self-determination was her thing, well, the flat was hers outright. She had the freehold. There were no strings, nothing that compromised her ownership. He had not done this to gain a hold over her, but to make her more secure. He had liberated her in the most fundamental way. Why couldn't she see it?

But the feeling that he was willing to go to such massive lengths to get his own way—and the ease with which he had achieved his ends—unnerved her in some fundamental way. She felt shaken, disturbed.

She already knew that a man who tried to undermine your self-determination was not to be trusted. In a wild flight of imagination, she realized that, stooping to tricks like that, it wouldn't be all that difficult for Jaf to get her pregnant. And then it would be her parents' story all over again.

So the first thing she did, when he gave her ownership of the fabulous flat, was show Jaf the door of it.

Lisbet sat for a moment, staring down at her own handwriting. After a moment she gathered up all the cheques. Then she sat with them in her hand, not looking at him.

''What was the message you intended me to take from this?'' Jaf demanded roughly.

At that her chin went up. ''This is the amount of

rent I had agreed to pay the owner to live in that apartment.''

''Well?''

Here, in this context, her actions suddenly seemed petty and ungenerous, even to herself. But it had not seemed that way in London, when each succeeding month in which he did not cash her cheques only made her more determined to make her point.

''No matter whose name is on the title deeds, the apartment is in fact owned by you,'' she said. ''I'm merely sticking by the deal I made before I moved in.''

''You knew there was no need,'' Jaf said.

''And you knew I felt there was a need! Why didn't you cash them?'' she demanded hotly. ''How do you think I felt about that? If we're talking about offending—''

''A need to repudiate my gift? Yes, I see. When did you meet Roger?''

''Ro—?'' Lisbet began in confusion, then gasped. She had almost fallen flat on her face. ''I'm not going to answer that.''

''Does he make love to you on the bed I bought for you? On the sheets that I gave you? Does he kiss you on the pillow where your head lay beside mine and we laughed? Is that why you sent me this *rent?*'' He flicked the little bundle in her hand. ''To salve your conscience for what you were doing?''

''This conversation is illuminating,'' she said brightly. ''It proves I was right, doesn't it? You manoeuvred me into that flat for one reason—to control me! Did you want me to feel too guilty and beholden ever to take another lover, Jaf? Our relationship was over. Should I have given up all other men forever because I was living in the flat you had manipulated me into? Or would a few years of celibacy have been enough for your ego? How many, exactly, would satisfy you?''

''I did not buy the flat to control you!'' He bit out every word.

''But having bought it, you're furious that it didn't have that effect?''

''Don't be a fool!''

''Meanwhile, here you were having a wonderful time with your gambling and your gold-plated Rolls. Isn't there a song that goes, 'You don't want me, but you want me to go on wanting you'?''

She held out the cheques.

''Please cash them,'' she said levelly. ''Thank you, but I don't like feeling like a kept woman.''

Jaf reached out and took the little bundle, ripped the cheques into pieces, pushed the window control again, and tossed the scraps into the wind. They whipped into a little whirlwind and then were lost against the vastness of the desert as she watched.

''If you send me another cheque, Lisbet,'' she heard him say in a dangerous voice, and her eyes moved to meet the black fury of his gaze, ''I will deposit a million pounds into your bank account. Then you will feel what it is to be a kept woman.''

They were approaching a small town, where a picturesque cluster of domed roofs sheltered in the protection of a palm forest. The limousine slowed and turned off the highway onto a rough, unpaved road. A few yards along, they pulled into the courtyard of a small building. There was a sign in Arabic script over the door.

"Is this where we're eating?" Lisbet exclaimed in surprise. She had been expecting that he would take her to one of the big expensive hotels, like the Sheikh Daud in Barakat al Barakat, where the producer had dined her on the first night of her arrival.

"The food is excellent," Jaf said, in a voice that said he had regained his self-control.

There was a tiny vestibule, and then the room they entered was dark, the walls and ceiling hung with swaths of exotic fabric and carpets in deep, rich shades. It was lighted with kerosene lamps, one on each of the low tables and a larger one hanging from the centre of each of the circles of fabric that draped the ceiling.

It was like entering a nomad's tent, quiet and mysterious. Lisbet smiled involuntarily as a dark-haired, heavyset woman came out through a curtained doorway with a cry of pleasure.

"*Marhaba!*" she cried, approaching Jaf with exuberant delight and stretching out her arms, then clapping her hands together and bowing her head in welcome, talking all the while. "*Assalaamu aleikum!*"

"*Waleikum assalaam, Umm Maryam.*"

They chatted like old friends for a moment, and then the hostess turned and smiled at Lisbet. "*Assalaamu aleikum. Ahlan wa sahlan!*"

"*Salaam aleikum,*" Lisbet returned with a smile, using up her entire cache of Arabic. But fortunately the woman didn't appear to expect any further response. She turned and led them along the room past several groups of diners who paused in their meal to stare, up two steps of a raised wooden platform at the end, and through a doorway in a partition of intricately arabesqued wood.

Lisbet reached out a hand to trace the birds and flowers frozen in permanent grace.

This area contained only two tables. With its lower ceiling, it felt enclosed and private. One kerosene lamp hung from the centre of the ceiling, giving subdued light. The hostess pulled out the low table to expose the cushions piled neatly on the floor and against the wall.

Lisbet sank down and Jaf slipped into a cross-legged posture beside her before helping to draw the table back into position.

Their hostess, meanwhile, lifted the lantern chimney and set a match to the wick. After a moment a little glow made the table their own special place.

Lisbet realized they were as intimate here as they could be anywhere.

"They have no printed menu," Jaf murmured, as the hostess disappeared. "Will you trust me to choose?"

She nodded.

His eyelids came down in lazy approval, and he smiled. "Good," he said, as if her permission had wider implications.

"My food, tonight," she told him evenly.

His nearness was making her skin hot. She could smell the scent of him, and she only had to close her eyes for that scent to take her back to moments whose memory melted her like a wax candle in a furnace. She lifted her chin and bit her lip to keep her eyes open, her guard up.

He looked as though he would have answered, but their hostess came through the little doorway with a tray. She set two generous glasses of rum-coloured liquid in front of them.

Lisbet picked it up and sipped. She blinked at the unexpected taste. "What is it?"

"Date juice with pine nuts," Jaf said, sipping his own. Lisbet took another sip, nodded and smiled at the hostess, miming enjoyment. Now she could recognize the flavour as dates. It was strange and different, but curiously pleasant.

Meanwhile, the woman, standing with the tray under one arm, was discussing the finer points of tonight's menu choices with Jaf. Lisbet listened absently to the strong Arabic consonants.

It felt odd to let him decide for her like this. But she was helpless without the language, and there was a strange comfort in having the decision taken out of her hands. It was almost like being a child—not that she had had much experience of that. Fate had given her an adult sense of responsibility very early.

"Do you like lamb?"

"As long as it's not a whole roast lamb, I can probably do justice to it."

"It's steak that's rolled and stuffed with dried fruits, herbs and spices, and baked in ashes. One of the specialties of the house, as well as being a traditional Barakati dish. No one does it better than Umm Maryam's mother."

"Her *mother?*"

"Yes, this is a family restaurant. Umm Maryam is the third generation. It was started by her grandmother."

Umm Maryam, understanding that she was under discussion, smiled at her. After a moment the meal negotiations drew to a close. The hostess made a couple of additional suggestions and Jaf nodded, and then with a smile she was gone.

The silence and peace of the place settled around them. Lisbet felt their mood change. Jaf seemed suddenly softened. His eyes lost their punishing glint.

"Do you come here much?" In London they had found several great little restaurants together, but if the newspapers were right, his tastes were very different here at home. Now it was only the most expensive, most popular *in* places for Sheikh Jafar al Hamzeh, whether they served good food or the place was hideously over-hyped.

"Would you have preferred to sample the night life of the city? We will do that after our meal."

"I wasn't lamenting the Sheikh Daud." Not by a long way. "I was just surprised."

He gave her a deliberate look, then spoke close to her ear. "I hope I will never lose the power to surprise you, Lisbet."

His voice caused little pilot lights of memory to puff into life, waiting for the signal to ignite her blood. He had said that once before. When she had been lying by his side, trembling in the aftermath of a pleasure so profound she had felt fundamentally changed. He had refused to stop until she was worn out.

"I think you just altered my DNA," she had murmured, half tranced with the mix of pleasure and sheer exhaustion. Every muscle twitched and trembled spasmodically.

That was when he had whispered it. *I hope I never lose the power to surprise you.* He'd said "hope," but his tone of voice had said he meant to make very sure of it.

She had responded only with a faint smile. Even her face muscles had been worked to overload.

Refusing to meet his eyes now, Lisbet shook off the

heaviness the memory provoked in her limbs. "You certainly surprised me today," she admitted waspishly. "What a mess you caused!"

Jaf lifted his eyebrows. "Was it so serious, what I did? It was only one scene."

"It was the master shot for a very difficult scene. Why did you do anything so crazy?"

A smiling young woman stepped through the doorway with their first course on a tray. She greeted Jaf with unabashed pleasure and set down several dishes to a rapid fire commentary before smiling shyly at Lisbet and disappearing.

"But I wanted to see you, Lisbet," Jaf murmured, picking up a large sprig of basil and munching it into his mouth bit by bit like a rabbit.

Which was totally inappropriate because, Lisbet was slowly coming to realize, with Jaf, *she* was the rabbit. The one who was hypnotized and then devoured whole.

# Five

"**T**here were easier ways," she said repressively, struggling to subdue her body's response to that simple statement. "You wrecked the day's filming. I don't know how much that little stunt will end up costing. No one could get back on form afterwards. You must have known it would cause disruption."

Jaf grinned. "Don't you know that I am mad, bad and dangerous to know?"

It was what a tabloid paper had called him a few weeks ago.

She took a mouthful of herb, watching him. "Why?"

He had taught her to eat the fresh herbs and bread in London, in the early, carefree days of their romance. Lisbet was surprised by the sharpness of memory that accompanied the taste on her tongue.

He grinned. "But for your sake, of course. I have gone mad for love, Lisbet."

"That's not what they say," she told him. "They say getting your hands on such a massive inheritance is what did it."

"Do they? Who says that?"

"Who doesn't say it?"

"Fools without romance," Jaf said dismissively.

He was being flippant; he didn't mean her to believe it. But there was an edge of something underneath the flippancy.

"Why are you courting publicity, Jaf?" she asked curiously.

He shrugged. "No Cup Companion has to court publicity, you know that. We are a natural resource."

It was true, but still, he had seemed to know exactly how to avoid being noticed when they wanted privacy in London. Now every move he made was reported. There had been a sea change in him.

"You may not have to, but today you certainly did."

"It won't do the film any harm." Jaf shrugged. "The prepublicity will probably be worth the price of a lost day's shooting, as I'm sure Masoud will see, once he's calmed down."

And then they were discussing the film, and suddenly the animosity between them died and it was like London again, with Jaf listening with the close interest he had always shown in anything that concerned her, and Lisbet confiding everything to him.

She was thrilled to be working with Masoud al Badi, a director whose last film had won the Palme d'Or at Cannes, and several other prestigious awards. This was a relatively low-budget film, but that was no problem, Lisbet told him, where there was a good script and good actors and no need for special effects and name stars.

And the part was brilliant, a perfect opportunity for her, if she had the talent to stretch to it. Lisbet was alternately terrified and thrilled at the challenge facing her.

"Why were you in the sea today? What is the story?"

"Don't you know about Rose Dumont, the bandit?"

"Tell me."

He had said that a couple of dozen times before. Jaf loved stories—he came from a nation of storytellers—and Lisbet had got into the habit of telling him the story of virtually every script that she read for.

"The screenplay is loosely based on her memoirs. Rose Dumont was the undutiful daughter of a rich London merchant. She didn't 'take' during her first social season, in about 1860, because she was too independent, too outspoken, and didn't suffer fools gladly. And she absolutely refused to go through the humiliation of a second season. So she was packed off by her family to India, where it was thought she would have a better chance of finding herself a husband."

"And did she look on it as an adventure?"

"She did. In her memoirs she wrote that she toyed with the idea of turning herself into a man on the ship, but she was too closely supervised to be able to put her plans into execution. Still, she was convinced that anything could happen, and she was right. She never got to India. Just off the coast of the Kingdom of Barakat, as it was in those days, Rose's ship was attacked by pirates. In the battle she was lost overboard. A piece of flotsam saved her.

"Rose got to shore—in the scene you interrupted today—and was immediately captured by a desert tribesman. But she put up such a powerful, spitting resistance to his advances that he got frightened that maybe she was one of the djinn—they're the people made of fire, you know, as humans are made from earth, and it can get tricky for humans to mess with them—and decided that instead of making her his own wife, he ought to offer her to the king."

Jaf scooped up another little cluster of herbs. "A djinn," he said thoughtfully, looking at Lisbet from lazy eyes, as if a new idea had occurred to him. "I never thought of that."

She ignored him. "Well, so he carried Rose to the palace and told the king he hadn't touched her, and the king accepted the gift, and Rose was dispatched to the harem. There she was left 'to languish among women' as she laments. Rose had always hated restriction, and she hated being in purdah. She wrote that she found life in the harem 'almost as limiting' as life in Victorian England," Lisbet reported with a grin.

She bent to pick up another morsel of hot flatbread with a little cube of goat's cheese, and set a sprig of herb on top before popping it into her mouth.

"She was bored, so she occupied her days learning Arabic—she had a quick ear and had whizzed through French and German in the schoolroom—and got fairly fluent.

"Most of the women in the harem were completely uneducated. But a few were very highly educated and skilled, and some, like herself, were foreign captives, and she allied herself with them. And between them these women began to plan an escape."

Jaf's eyebrows went up. "Where did they think they would go?"

"They bribed one of the eunuchs, and he agreed to help them. Bit by bit he took their valuables and jewels to the market and sold them. With the proceeds, when they had enough, they planned to buy a boat and hire a captain. They were going to set sail and take their luck."

"Very courageous," Jaf interjected, his eyebrows still up.

"In the middle of all this, something happened. After almost two years, one night the king suddenly remembered the gift the desert tribesman had brought to him, the foreign woman with the unusual colouring, and he sent to the harem for her."

Jaf gave her a look. "Lucky king, to have such power," he murmured.

Lisbet had to close her eyes. She swallowed. "Rose doesn't go into detail for her Victorian audience, but she does obliquely hint that she had learned certain skills from the eunuchs. 'I took Queen Esther as my guide,' she wrote. Maybe you know that Esther learned tricks from the eunuchs that allowed her to impress Ahasuerus, the King of the Medes and Persians, when she was finally summoned to his bed."

"I have not heard this story before."

"It's in the Bible," Lisbet said. "Ahasuerus is called Artaxerxes in the history books. Anyway, whatever Rose actually did that night, and on succeeding nights, the king fell in love with her, eventually becoming completely besotted with her."

"Of course."

Lisbet pressed her lips together and resisted her response to his teasing. "Do you want to hear this story or not?"

Jaf's eyebrows shot up again. "What am I doing wrong?"

"Never mind. Just don't interrupt so much, okay?"

Obediently he closed his mouth, but there was still a wicked glint in his eyes. Lisbet shook her head and looked away to take another bite of food.

"Rose suddenly found herself in the position of being the king's favourite, and life in the harem changed dramatically for her. She had power. She got a new apartment in the harem. She gave birth to a son, and received even more honours. She began to get gifts from people who wanted her to intercede for them with the king.

"This was a great advantage, because it meant the women could sell the stuff and make their escape that much sooner. And then one day, just when their plans were reaching fruition, Rose made the discovery that she was happier than she had ever been, right where she was.

"She had fallen in love with the king. They would talk long into the night about everything from affairs of state to astronomy. He consulted her and listened to her. She'd never met her intellectual match in a man before, and here he was. And she had a lovely baby son. Rose was enjoying life more than ever before.

"The other women were still desperate to escape, of course. And so Rose was faced with a choice."

She paused, and Jaf shook his head.

"A choice? What was there to choose? She had a husband and a child. What could weigh against that?"

Lisbet looked at him. "He wasn't her husband, Jaf, he was her owner. And the alternative was freedom."

She saw fury blaze in his eyes.

At that moment, the smiling young woman arrived with their second course, the lamb. A wonderful aroma came with her, and it was so mouth-watering that Lisbet completely lost track of her story.

"Ohhh, it smells delicious!" she cried, as a plate was set before her. The meat practically disintegrated at one touch of her fork, and the scent of the mix of herbs and spices was out of this world.

For a few minutes they ate in silence, for in the Barakat Emirates eating is a serious business and there is no social compulsion to make conversation over a meal. When conversation began again they talked mostly about the food. But when the main course had been cleared away, Jaf returned to the story of the film.

"You were telling me about Rose," he said.

After much soul-searching, Rose had decided to escape with the other women.

"She knew that one day she would fall out of favour with the king. Her happiness was entirely dependent on his will. She wanted to have a life where she controlled her own destiny. And she felt she couldn't disappoint all her friends who had worked and planned for so long.

"The day came when the eunuch returned to the palace to report that the boat and a captain were ready. The eunuch had arranged the departure for a date when the tide would be going out early in the morning, so the women could escape by night and go straight aboard.

"On the appointed night the women collected in Rose's apartments, where they dressed in men's clothing. When the palace was asleep, the women kissed their sleeping children and prepared to go."

''They didn't take their children?''

''They couldn't. It would have been too much of a risk. Rose says she almost relented as she bent over her sleeping son and kissed him for the last time.''

''This must be fiction. Do you believe this, Lisbet? That a woman leaves her child for such a reason? Could you do such a thing?''

''They were in a situation they hadn't asked for, Jaf. They hadn't come to the harem willingly, had they? None of them went to the king's bed voluntarily.''

''Except Rose.''

She ignored that. ''The eunuch let them out of the harem and led them by secret ways out of the palace and into the city. They trooped down to the shore, but when they got there, the eunuch mysteriously disappeared.''

''Ah.''

''Yes. The captain of the boat matching the description the eunuch had given to Rose denied all knowledge. They had been betrayed. Rose never was certain whether it was the eunuch's doing, or whether the eunuch himself had been taken in by the captain, and murdered under cover of night as they crept along.

''But the sun was coming up and they had no time to think about it. As soon as the alarm was raised in the palace they would be searched out and put to death. Rose had brought her remaining jewels with her, and they used them to buy horses and weapons. And instead of escaping by sea, they fled inland, into the desert. Eventually, she and a number of women managed to set up camp in a ruin by an oasis.''

Jaf looked faintly incredulous. ''And they survived there?''

''They became bandits, rivalling the notorious Abu

Tariq, who controlled a huge slice of the Barakati desert. He was the grandfather of the Selim who was grandfather of ex-Prince Jalal, by the way.''

Jaf's eyebrows climbed into his hair. "And how did Rose manage to survive in a desert controlled by the great Abu Tariq?"

"She says that after one encounter Abu Tariq left them alone, and they had an unspoken agreement to divide the desert in such a way that Rose was left exclusive control over a small territory. She doesn't say exactly how they came to that agreement, but it's possible she used the same arts she'd used on the king. Some historians have suggested that Rose gave birth to the man who was later the father of Selim."

Jaf smiled. "Is this being billed as a true story?"

Lisbet believed it, or most of it, but she only shrugged. "It's what Rose published in her memoirs. Some people at the time debunked her story, too, but then in 1958 someone did some research on the story in Barakat and found references to a band of women bandits in the desert at that period.

"They were noted for their ferocity, apparently. The records say the women had control over a certain segment of the caravan routes. People used to double the guard over that part of the route, because the women bandits terrified people even more than Abu Tariq's gang.

"And they are mentioned as having been finally wiped out in about 1890, which is the date Rose gives for her return to England."

"She returned?"

"She got homesick in middle age. So she passed leadership of the gang over to a younger deputy, and travelled back to the port with one sidekick. She saw a European traveller, and robbed him of his baggage. Then she passed herself off as an Englishman. She had plenty of valuables to barter for passage back to England, the proceeds of her bandit life.

"Her memoirs are fascinating, but she doesn't go into as much detail as I'd like. The book was hugely popular reading among women for a decade or so, and she was a heroine, but her story was pooh poohed a lot. There were discrepancies in it."

"What did she do, back in England?"

"Took up the cause of women's votes, of course!" Lisbet laughed. "Actually her life wasn't by any means over. In the First World War, when she was quite old but still very fit, she worked as a battlefield nurse. She died in the flu epidemic of 1919."

"Alone, and childless."

"Yes, but the film doesn't end there."

"How does it end?"

"On her deathbed, Rose remembers a particular moment in her bandit life. It's not in her memoirs—the story has been changed quite a bit for the film. She and a few of her band come upon a young man who's become separated from a hunting party. He defends himself so bravely for one so young that they decide to take him prisoner.

"Then the king and his companions ride to the rescue, and the bandits realize that he is the Crown Prince. Rose suddenly understands that the boy is her own son. So it's very poignant, because she sees her other life—the might have been. She would have been mother of the Crown Prince, perhaps mother of the king one day. Without identifying herself, she demands the young prince's sword as ransom, releases him and gallops off with her women."

"And the king lets her go?" Jaf asked.

"He doesn't recognize her."

Jaf was shaking his head. "Impossible," he said.

She bit her lip. "Why is it impossible?"

"How could he fail to recognize the woman he had loved?"

"Fifteen or sixteen years," she pointed out weakly.

He reached out to stroke that tiny tuft of hair that just hugged her temple. "Even a hundred years would not be enough to wipe away the sound of your voice, Lisbet, the scent of you, the way the colour of your eyes changes with your mood." He dropped his hand.

"A man may stop loving, but he can never forget."

### Sheikh Jaf's Film Flam

Jafar al Hamzeh, bad boy Cup Companion to Prince Karim, apparently wants to be a movie star, and he believes in taking the direct route. Yesterday the handsome sheikh galloped onto the set of Masoud al Badi's latest film while a scene was being filmed in the Barakati desert, threw the English star, Lisbet Raine, over his saddle, and...

Lisbet tossed the paper down without reading any more, stood restlessly and moved to the little trolley to pour herself a cup of coffee. She stood sipping as she gazed at the scene around her.

The house, high on a forested escarpment that lined this arm of the bay, faced south along a white sand beach and curving shoreline. It was a fabulous view, and the air was wonderful. A soft breeze rippled the skirt of her turquoise sundress against her calves. Mental cobwebs didn't stand a chance here.

"You're staying with us, of course," her friend

Anna had said. She was the first person, after her mother, whom Lisbet had called to give the news that she had landed the female lead in Masoud al Badi's latest film and would be coming to Barakat to do the location shooting. "It'll be wonderful to have you for a long visit."

Lisbet was thrilled to be here in Anna's new home, of course, but there was pain mingled with the pleasure. To see Gazi and Anna so happy in their marriage, planning a future together, was lovely. But every intimate smile they exchanged, every quick, loving touch, reminded her that this was something she herself might have had, if only...

But she had made the right choice, even if not for the right reasons. Jaf wasn't Gazi, a fact the newspapers delighted in pointing out. He didn't have his brother's stability. Life with Jaf would have been no more secure than life with her father. Last night had proved that.

"Good morning!"

Anna was leaning over the flower-covered balcony above. As Lisbet looked up, blinking in the sunlight, Anna lifted a hand in greeting and then turned and started down the beautiful, centuries-old stone staircase.

When she arrived on the terrace the two friends kissed and exchanged morning chitchat as Anna poured herself coffee and sat down in the delicious shade of the huge umbrella that protected the table.

Her eyes fell on the headline, and she made a little face. "What's Jaf been doing?"

"You haven't heard about yesterday yet?" Lisbet had arrived back with Jaf very late, when the household was already asleep.

"I know Gazi got a phone call from Jaf that had him hopping."

"Was he trying to suppress the story? Wasted effort."

"Gazi can do most things when it comes to publicity," Anna said, bridling a little. "But I know with Jaf damage limitation is difficult. The press really love to write about his escapades."

Lisbet blew on her coffee and sipped. "Well, and there are moles on any movie, and mobile phones work out there. Within half an hour of Jaf galloping onto the set, half a dozen journalists at least had the story."

She nodded at the stack of newspapers on the end of the table. "Wonderful how he timed the stunt just in time for the Sunday gossip glut."

Anna opened her eyes. "Jaf galloped onto the set?"

"Rode his white steed into the middle of a scene we were shooting, chased me down the beach when I freaked and ran, did a flying pickup that could have killed us both, and kept on going, with me clinging on for dear life. You'll catch flies like that," Lisbet advised her friend in a matter-of-fact voice.

Anna's lower jaw was halfway to her chest. "You—he—what? I don't believe it!" she babbled, though she clearly did, every word. Her hand reached mechanically for the tabloid with the screaming headline.

"Hey, you're checking my story against the *Sunday Mirror?*" Lisbet chided with mock indignation. "*I'm* the eyewitness!"

But Anna couldn't tear her eyes away from the story, which was illustrated by a fuzzy long shot of a galloping horseman. It might or might not have been a still from yesterday's film.

"Oh, I wonder how Gazi's going to feel about this! Everyone knows Prince Karim's warned Jaf to stop courting publicity." She looked up. "If he's stripped of his title, it will be a deep family shame, you know."

"Is it likely?"

Anna shrugged.

"This isn't exactly a hanging offence, is it?" Lisbet found herself saying. "Now that I've cooled down about it, I begin to see that he's done us a big favour. I'm sure a film doesn't often get prepublicity as good as this."

Anna laughed. "Maybe you should have married him, after all. He could make you famous."

"Thanks. In those immortal, always relevant words, I'd rather do it myself."

"Sorry, darling, of course you would!" Anna's eyes dropped to the story. She read for a moment, then gasped on laughter. "Did you really refuse to work as long as Jaf was on the set?"

"I was pretty peeved," Lisbet admitted.

"'The actress was, in effect, throwing the wealthy sheikh off his own land. The producers may count themselves lucky that he has not returned the favour. The movie location is being leased from the arts-loving Cup Companion at a nominal sum,'" Anna read aloud.

She tossed aside the paper as a servant silently approached across the tiled courtyard. "Morning, Mansour. What would you like for breakfast, Lisbet?"

"Let's have something lazy. I'm not called today."

When breakfast had been decided on, Anna stood up and moved to where a dozen European newspapers were neatly stacked at the end of the table. She flipped through them.

"Not many have actually put it on the front page. They're more concerned with the drugs pipeline." She held up the *Times* for Lisbet to read the headline.

*Barakati Heroin Connection Baffles Scotland Yard.*

Anna picked up the *Sunday Mirror* again. "This looks like the worst one," she said, and slipped it well down in the pile. "That way Gazi doesn't have to see it first thing," she said, smiling conspiratorially at Lisbet. "Let him concentrate on the heroin. It's less personal."

Lisbet's heart gave one spasmodic beat. It must be nice to care about someone like that, wanting to protect them.

"Jaf came in with me last night, by the way. He said it was too far to go home."

"I know he spent the night here. He's with Gazi in his office right now."

"Is Gazi very worried about him?"

Anna sat down again. "He doesn't say much about it. He reads every story that's printed, but when I try to get him to open up—" She shrugged.

"Does he talk to Jaf about it?"

"Not in front of me. I don't know what they're discussing now. As you saw, Jaf hasn't been here for a while."

"Oh, he said that was on my account," Lisbet said.

"Really? I must admit I was a little surprised. I thought he'd come the moment he knew you were here."

"I told you he wouldn't," Lisbet said quietly. Still, she had spent the week in unconscious expectation. Maybe that was why she had been so thrown by Jaf's appearance on the beach. There had to be some reason for the blind panic that had descended on her when she looked up and saw his face.

"Sometimes I wonder if all this would be happening if you had married Jaf," Anna commented, shaking her head. "It was when he got back here after you two broke up that all this started to happen, you know. Sometimes I wish—"

Lisbet lifted a hand to stop her friend. "Then he must have been pretty unstable in the first place, Anna. Don't wish it on me. I don't want to be anyone's sole moral support. And if you'd seen what I saw last night…"

"How was dinner?"

"Dinner was fine. It was the gambling afterwards that really opened my eyes. We went to the Shalimar Gardens."

The Shalimar Gardens, as Lisbet had quickly learned, was an extremely luxurious casino, recently built on the grounds of the Sheikh Daud hotel for the entertainment of wealthy foreign tourists. It was one of only two casinos in the country.

"Oh, damn," Anna said softly. "Oh, Lisbet, please don't mention that to Gazi! What happened?"

"He gambled, he popped champagne, he tipped wildly, he lost."

"How much?"

"I have no idea. A fortune. He was just a totally different person. A caricature. I hated the whole scene."

"Shhhh!" Anna hissed sharply. "Here they come."

Lisbet turned her head. The two brothers, in light-coloured shorts and dark polo shirts, were just emerg-

ing from the house. Both had strong bodies and powerfully muscled legs with fine, bony ankles.

Jaf was laughing at something Gazi had just said,
his head thrown back. The sun burnished his thick,
ruffled hair and darkly tanned skin.

"Cor! They are a gorgeous pair, aren't they?" Lisbet exclaimed, in stage Cockney.

"Phwooah," Anna agreed.

When they arrived at the table, Gazi bent to kiss his
wife, his hand cupping her head with an intimate, protective hold that made Lisbet bite her lip and look
away.

Jaf headed for the coffee trolley, poured himself a
cup, turned and looked straight into her eyes. His gaze
had an unreadable glint. Her heart kicked a little pro-
test as he approached, but he only pulled out a chair
on her right and slipped into it.

"So, have you told Roger all about your date with
your ex-lover?" he asked.

Anna's interest was instantly caught. She glanced
over, but the warning in Lisbet's eyes stopped her curious question in her throat. Lisbet couldn't be sure
whether Jaf had intercepted the look or not.

"I just got up," she protested.

Jaf laughed. "In that case, why not save the con-
fession till tonight? Might as well be hanged for a
sheep as a lamb. Let me show you a bit of the country
today."

# Six

---

It was a beautiful country, as he had promised. First he took her to the Bostan al Sa'adat—The Garden of Joy—where inside a high wall enclosing several acres of land there were fountains and canals, and every kind of plant and tree and bird imaginable. It was very peaceful.

"Boy, they knew something about stress relief, didn't they?" Lisbet marvelled.

"This garden was endowed by King Daud over sixty years ago, at the time of his marriage to his beautiful, foreign first wife," Jaf told her as they wandered behind a tiny waterfall. "It took twenty years to complete."

Then they visited the fifteenth-century Great Mosque, and the tomb of Queen Halimah, in the city centre, said to be among the most perfect surviving examples of classical Islamic architecture in the world.

It was the first time Lisbet had ever seen anything so beautiful up close. Her mouth was permanently open with wonder.

At the entrance to one room, which was completely covered in a mosaic of tiny mirrored tiles, she paused, breathless with astonishment.

The room was filled with light that had no discernible source. The room simply glowed, as if endless reflection were enough in itself to produce light.

"It's like being in the centre of a diamond!" Lisbet whispered.

She wondered if he was remembering all the times he had described these architectural wonders to her, and promised that one day he would bring her here. She certainly could not forget. It had happened mostly when they lay in bed after lovemaking. They were always close at such times, and his descriptions of the wonders she would see became a part of the soft lovers' chat they shared.

But if it bothered him that, though he was showing these things to her as he had promised, they were no longer lovers, he gave no sign.

He drove her out into the desert, where they visited an ancient ruin so worn by time it might almost have been a natural geographical feature. Lisbet was entranced again, for a completely different reason.

"This must be just the kind of place Rose Dumont and her women took refuge in! They had an oasis, though, of course."

There was no water here. The arched, crumbling, mud-brick walls were as dry as the sand dust that blew against them. The ruin was a potent reminder of the limited importance of individual lives.

"'My name is Ozymandias, king of kings,'" she

recited. "'Look on my works, ye Mighty, and despair.'"

"No one even knows that much," Jaf said. "There is no king's name here."

"How old is it?" she demanded, walking around every inch of the walls and trying to imagine the people who had lived here. The sun burned down on the empty vastness that surrounded them, making the air dance. Lisbet thought she could almost see the ghost of the original building in the shimmer.

Jaf shook his head. "It's virtually impossible to date such a ruin accurately. Mud brick was used for millennia. And arches, too, go back to earliest times. All identifying detail has been worn away by time."

She stood under one crumbling arch, looking out over the endless stretch of desert. A light wind blew the long skirt of her rich aquamarine dress, grabbed at the broad brim of the protective hat she wore.

"Someone stood here once," she told him, in an imaginative half-trance. "I can almost feel her. She stood here looking out over the desert while a storm blew, waiting for someone to come back."

What a harsh, inhospitable land this was, but it had enormous drawing power. Its magnetism was a tangible thing.

"Just like a sailor's sweetheart, waiting and praying was all she could do. But for her the sea and the storm were made of sand."

"And did he come back?" Jaf asked, in a low, rough voice.

The whisper of heartbreak seemed to touch her mind. "I don't know," Lisbet murmured, shaking her head to try to free herself of the strange impression. "Maybe not."

"And still she waits," he said. "You feel her presence after hundreds, perhaps thousands of years. How can *you* sense the mind of such a woman, you who waited no more than weeks? Do you claim to have a heart that understands such loyalty?"

Her breath trembled at the passion his voice struggled with. Against her will her heart caught fire. Her lips were dry. She couldn't speak.

"What have you done to us, Lisbet?" he demanded, his voice quiet, but intense enough for a brand. "What have you destroyed, with your foolish resistance? I loved you enough for a dozen lifetimes, but that was not enough for you. What did you want, Lisbet? What more did you want, that you were so eager to kill my love?"

She tried to swallow, but her throat closed.

"Look at me."

It would be fatal to look at him in this mood, she knew it. Lisbet kept her eyes firmly on the distant dunes, where the early-afternoon sun was already painting faint shadows. How mysterious the desert was, with its ripples and waves. Like a solidified sea.

"Look at me, Lisbet," he commanded again. He was close beside her now, his voice against her ear. He lifted a hand to her chin and drew her head around to face him.

"I didn't want *anything* from you!" she cried furiously, finding her voice at last. "I told you, what I wanted was to be free to be myself. You wanted to own me, and I didn't w—"

In furious silence his mouth smothered hers. Liquid fire seared her lips, sending a spear of flame along every limb, and into her heart—a stabbing, sudden heat as powerful as the first time they had kissed, almost a year ago.

It was a punishing, tormenting, hungry kiss, but irresistibly it summoned up her own wild, half-buried hunger. With a helpless moan she opened her mouth under the onslaught of his, and his tongue pushed into the moist cavity savagely, ferociously, driving a storm of desire pell-mell into her blood.

It lasted moments only. With the same suddenness, Jaf lifted his mouth, and his arms fell away. Lisbet closed her eyes against the rush of emptiness.

"The wind is blowing harder," he said in a harsh voice. "We'd better get back to the city."

"Coffee, Ahmad, and would you toast me one of those, please?" Lisbet said, pointing.

Behind her in the canteen tent, conversation was picking up again. It had parted like the Red Sea when Lisbet appeared, and no prizes for guessing what everyone had been discussing.

She picked up her coffee cup and toasted bun with a murmur of thanks and, giving a little general wave, stepped out into the early-morning sunshine to walk slowly back to her trailer. Sometimes she ate her breakfast in the canteen, but not today. She would only put a crimp in the conversation.

Tina was already waiting in her trailer, nursing her own cup of coffee.

"How was your date?"

"We ate, and then we went to the casino," Lisbet replied shortly, sinking into a chair as she pried the plastic lid off the cup. Yesterday's *Mirror* newspaper lay on the table. *Film Flam.* What a ridiculous play on words.

Taking a bite of her toasted Danish, Lisbet licked her fingers and picked up her coffee.

"The casino?" Tina demanded.

"The Shalimar Gardens. Very, very," Lisbet murmured, waving her hand expressively.

"Did he win? Did you play?"

"No, twice."

"Wow, not even one bet?"

"Jaf was leaving enough behind for both of us."

"I guess you saw the story," Tina said, nodding towards the paper as she zipped open a garment bag.

Lisbet nodded.

Her costume was lifted out of the bag and hung; the same one as on Saturday.

Lisbet set down her coffee cup and picked up a tissue to wipe the butter from her fingers. She stood up.

"Have you got the right costume? I thought we got that scene in the can Saturday."

"That's not what the call sheet says this morning," Tina told her.

"Was there a problem with the rushes?" If there was a problem, it had something to do with Jaf and the way he had stormed the set, she was sure. But she decided not to suggest it to Tina.

The dresser shrugged expressively. "Mine not to reason why."

"Damn." Lisbet shook her head. "I hope I'm not going to have to do that water thing again."

There was a tap on the door, and the director entered on her call. "I'll be retaking some of the close-up and medium shots today, Lisbet," he said.

"So I hear," she said. "What happened, Masoud?"

He scratched behind his ear. "We're going to be doing it with a white horse."

"A white horse!" she repeated, surprised.

"The scene will be slightly different, too. You run from Adnan when he rides up and he gallops after you and picks you up."

She gazed at the director. "Do you mean you're going to shoot something like what actually happened when Jaf—"

"It looked very good in the rushes. Very, very good. The white horse—everything looked very good. We want to capture that chemistry if we can."

Stunt people, of course, were doing the close-ups of the actual pickup. Lisbet spent the morning kicking her heels while the scene between her and Jaf was played and replayed for the cameras.

The afternoon was spent largely on one sequence. This entailed Lisbet leaping up from the sand and running along the shore while she turned and shrieked defiance over her shoulder, pursued, first, by the cameraman on a dune buggy, second, by the cameraman on the back of the white horse, and third, by Adnan on the horse and the cameraman on the dune buggy behind him.

It was a high-spirited horse, and at various times it took exception to Lisbet's curses, her hair, the camera, a grip, the clapboard, the dune buggy, and anything else that came in its way. And every time it did it spoiled the shot.

Lisbet lost count of the times she started up and plunged along the beach, only to hear the calm cry of "cut" behind her.

And after each attempt, someone had to come and

rake the sand clear of footprints, hoof marks, and wheel treads, and pump seawater to smooth it down.

Each time Lisbet retreated to the shade of an umbrella to have sunblock reapplied and drink ice water while she waited for the next take. Since her costume tended to dry on her within a very few minutes, it had to be damped down before each take.

The afternoon was tedium itself.

But no one thought of complaining, least of all Lisbet. Masoud al Badi was a brilliant director, and he was known for his moments of inspired madness on the set. If anything, she felt honoured to be part of a vision she could not understand.

By the time Masoud was satisfied, Lisbet had run herself nearly into heat exhaustion, her skin felt toasted, and her voice was hoarse. She collapsed into the dune buggy and was chauffeured up to her trailer. "Just throw me under the shower and turn it on," she said to Tina as her dresser worked on the thousand tiny buttons running down the back of her costume.

"There's no water," Tina warned her, grimacing apologetically. "Someone forgot to bring in the truck yesterday, and no one realized it till the tank ran dry an hour ago. They've called for an emergency supply, but it won't be here for at least an hour."

So when Jaf showed up a few minutes later suggesting drinks and dinner at his house, Lisbet didn't put up any argument at all.

"The sky here is just the way you described it," Lisbet smiled, leaning back to look up at the stars as they walked along the beach.

"Did I tell you about the sky?" Jaf murmured, as if he had forgotten.

She knew she was a fool to be disappointed. Why should he remember now, when he no longer loved her? Maybe someone else's skin was his velvet sky now.

"Once, you did," she said.

The limousine had driven again in the direction of Umm Maryam's restaurant, then along the side road through the forest of date palms, till the road came to an end at a high white wall and a massive pair of gates.

His house was even more beautiful than his descriptions of it, long months ago in England. Like many homes here, it was built around a central courtyard with a pool and fountain. The courtyard was partially latticed over to protect against the harsh sun, and the branches of trees had been trained over the lattice, giving a delicious, dappled shade.

Dinner was served in a long room with arched windows overlooking the courtyard, and paved with a mosaic in a carpet design of the most intricate workmanship, in pink, brown, black, red and white marble.

Jaf's conversation had been only slightly barbed, keeping her on edge without actually attacking her.

For their coffee they moved out under the stars beside the pool, where the fountain burbled gently in the darkness. The pattern of glazed tiles on the floor and the raised sides of the pool had been worn by the passage of centuries, but was perhaps more beautiful in age than it had ever been.

The air was perfumed by flowers. A night bird sang. It was as idyllic as he had promised.

Except that he did not love her.

After coffee, Jaf took some cubes of sugar in his hand and they went out to the stables. Firouz pushed his head eagerly against his master's chest, accepted the small sweet tribute. A mare, too, put her head over the stable gate and whinnied softly.

"Oh, aren't you a pretty one?" Lisbet crooned, stroking the soft nose.

"Shall we ride?" Jaf asked. It was another of the things he had told her they would do, in London. Lisbet couldn't resist the beauty of the night, and five minutes later, bareback, barefoot, they were riding down towards the sea.

They galloped along the water's edge, then dismounted and, dropping the reins, left the horses and walked splashing through the cool water as the waves whispered up the sand.

The stars were breathtaking, and so numerous it was difficult to pick out the major constellations from among the wild sparkle. And Lisbet was reminded of the moment when he had described the night sky and the stars to her. A moment he had forgotten.

"It sounded like something out of a dream," she said. It seemed like a dream now, the rich, sensuous purple-black, so spangled with glittering lights. *So soft your fingers long to touch it,* he had said.

"How did I describe it to you?" Jaf prodded gently, and Lisbet bit back a rueful smile and shook her head. She was a fool to have let him see how much she remembered.

"I said that your skin was like the night sky," he said, in a rough, purring voice. "Didn't I? Velvet, so that one longed to touch it. Is that what I said?"

His voice brought back the physical memory so sharply she choked on a gasp, remembering how he had stretched out beside her, stroking her trembling body to quiescence after half killing her with sexual pleasure.

*Beautiful,* he had breathed, running one strong, sensitive hand along her quivering thigh. *Only the night sky in Barakat is as soft as your skin, Lisbet.* And then he had told her about his grandfather's diamonds.

Now her skin was melting with the memory, with the heat of the evening, the burn of his voice. She closed her eyes. ''Yes,'' she whispered, ''that's what you said.'' And now she was burning up with yearning.

''Your soul, too, I described, do you remember?''

She couldn't answer. The pressure in her throat was almost intolerable, and she didn't know what would come out if she parted her lips.

''I said your soul was pure and burning, like the stars, isn't that what I said?''

She bowed her head, and if he wanted to take it as a nod, he could.

''How wrong I was, Lisbet. But I am not the first man to be blinded by beauty.''

A breeze caressed her bare legs and shoulders, stirred her hair, and sensations of painful delight quivered through her, as if the wind were his body and arms.

''You remember it—our time together?'' he demanded, as if the question were torn from him. ''You remember what I said to you, how you responded?''

Lisbet bit her lip in the attempt to keep her emotions at bay.

''You remember,'' he murmured in a rough, tortured voice. ''You can remember such love, and then lie to me about belonging to another man.''

She gasped.

''You are surprised. But such a shallow, empty lie, Lisbet—why should it have convinced me for longer than a day? Why did you say it? Were you so afraid of my love? But there is nothing to fear anymore.''

She opened her mouth on a soundless sigh.

''You have come to my home, where I dreamed of seeing you, where I knew that our love would reach perfection. But you come too late. How can it be that you are here at last only when my love is ashes in my mouth?''

She looked at him, not understanding the pang that pierced her. This was what she wanted, wasn't it? Freedom to be herself. To be alone.

''Then what are we doing here?'' she asked, her voice catching in her throat.

He laughed, but without joy. ''I did not say I do not want you. That did not die with my love. I want to make love to you, Lisbet,'' he said with rough urgency. ''It is like thirst in the desert.''

And he would know. His voice caressed her like silken water, his need beat upon her like waves, drowning her in the flood tide of her own need to love and be loved by him.

''My arms long to hold you, my mouth to taste you, Lisbet. My hunger is the hunger of a thousand wolves. But now it is the kind of wanting you wanted me to feel. It is wanting without a heart. Isn't it so? Now you will be happy, even though such love is a travesty. Let us make love on this new bargain. We will mate as animals, thinking of nothing but pleasure.''

''Jaf,'' she pleaded. ''You know—''

He was suddenly fiercely angry. ''No!'' he rasped. ''I know nothing!'' He wrapped his arms around her in passionate abandon, and she felt his mouth ravage hers. His wild, angry passion thrilled through her like flame, burning up everything except hunger.

"Jaf," she moaned, on fire for him.

"Say it!" he commanded. "Tell me it is all you want!"

The world tilted, and somehow she was on the sand underneath his long, hard body, the stars a wild curtain of diamonds above their heads. On the horizon a fat orange moon was lifting out of the water, pouring liquid red-gold over the shifting ripples, colouring it till it looked like the desert sand.

His touch was everywhere. Where his hands grasped her, her flesh grew hot, her blood thundered. "Tell me!"

It was impossible to resist him any longer. His wildness infected her at the deepest level of being.

And as if his anguished passion were a burning brand setting her alight, now, at last, Lisbet recognized the love she had hidden deep inside. Set free by the flames of the remorse and regret that swept her, as surely as if he had burnt down a prison that held her, love stood up without disguise for the first time.

She was breathless with the discovery, and with the anguish of knowing that it had come too late.

"Tell me!" he cried again, and the torment in him was like fuel on the flames, so that it seemed that soon there would be nothing in the world but love.

But what she wanted to tell him now, he no longer wanted to hear.

# Seven

**H**e lay over her, his hand stroking her with a trembling caress, rough and urgent against her arm, her breast, her hip, her cheek. Then his fingers locked in her hair, his eyes lost the glint of starshine, and she had only time for the tiniest indrawn breath before his mouth smothered hers.

His body came down hard against her now, angry, urgent, punishing, passionate. His sex pressed painfully against her groin. His kiss pushed into her mouth, starving, ruthless.

Her fingers locked in his thick hair and she pulled her mouth away from his, gasping against an upsurge of need that swamped her. Was this what she had feared? This deep, unrelenting passion? She moaned with the hopeless understanding that had come too late.

"This I can give you," he said hoarsely, hearing

her cry. "This is what you want from me. Show me how much you want it, Lisbet!"

He let her go to kneel above her on the damp sand of their bed. She was weeping with need, with the hunger of long months, with the joy of discovery and the pain of loss. She called his name desperately, not the Jaf who was with her now, but the Jaf she had known, the man who had loved her and offered his heart without reserve.

"I am here," he answered roughly, dragging up her skirt so that the moonlight painted her legs and hips, outlining the tiny sliver of lace that was all that barred her body from him. Of their own accord his fingers caught the lace and drew it down her legs and away.

With quiet ferocity he pushed her thighs apart and bent down between them, grasping her hips. His mouth tasted her flesh, and his hands felt the quivering response.

He knew her so well. He knew every inch of her, every atom. All that she was. She had closed her heart and her throat on the words he had wanted to hear, but she could not now refuse him her body's response.

His tongue found the tender bud, his mouth enclosed her in warmth. His hands clasped her thighs' smooth muscle. He felt the pleasure he made for her build in hungry ripples, felt her fingers clench in his hair. Heard her breathing quicken to a moan.

He lifted his head. "Oh!" she cried in soft disappointment.

"Tell me, Lisbet," he said. "Is this what you want?"

"Jaf," she protested on a sigh. She both wanted and did not want it. She wanted the loving Jaf she had known. Now that his heart was no longer hers for the asking, she saw what a jewel she had spurned.

He lowered his head again. Stroked and rasped her with his determined, angry tongue. Tendrils of fire curled out from under his mouth, honey melted under his fingertips to spread sweetness through her body under her skin.

His hands stroked the tender skin, kneaded the flesh of her thighs, her abdomen, her hips, and every touch sent heat and delight shivering through her. His mouth, his tongue, toyed and toyed with her pleasure, building it by the slowest imaginable stages.

No effort was necessary, no clenching or straining. He knew her body perfectly. She felt her pleasure slowly tense, like a wild animal preparing to leap, and then, without effort, it was there, spiralling and flooding through her, the sweet, sweet burning that only he could give her.

"This is what I offer you now, Lisbet. Is it what you want?"

"Jaf!"

His hand stroked her moon-kissed abdomen, molten gold turning to silver-gilt as the moon climbed higher up the sky behind his head. His elbows kept her legs apart, opening her to his eyes and his kiss. She was half fainting with hunger for him to complete what was begun.

His mouth lowered again, and he smiled at the convulsive tightening in her thighs. The suddenness of his heat and his tongue drew her breath in on a tiny gasp, but he heard it even against the shushing of the surf, and it was like whiskey in his blood.

A larger wave frothed up the sand, running under his feet and legs and up under her knees, adding the water's contribution to her fever. Her hips lifted, seeking the release that his mouth promised. She moaned a tiny moan, like soft wind against a rock, and it burst in her again, an explosion of molten delight. Her body arched and trembled, and sank down again onto the sand.

She locked her fingers in his hair and tried to pull him up into her embrace. He lifted his head, and she felt his dark gaze touch her, though the moonlight blinded her.

"Say it, Lisbet," he commanded, his voice rasping her nerve endings as surely as, a moment ago, his tongue had.

"Jaf, please!"

"Yes, I please. I will, Lisbet. Only tell me, and I will do all that you desire and more."

"What do you want to hear?" she cried, knowing the answer.

"That in this way, if no other, you are mine."

The plain, flat statement was loaded with hunger and possession, and her response sliced through her like a newly sharpened sword. She turned her head helplessly from side to side.

"What do you want to prove?" she pleaded.

"When it is true, you will tell me," he said, and his mouth came down again.

Pleasure rippled through her body, pleasure like a thousand silver bells on a string pulled into shivery motion by his touch. Their delicate tinkling music built to a slow clamour in her blood, and she was wild for the deafening crescendo when it came.

His tongue rasped along her abdomen, brushed down a thigh, then to her inner thigh, tormenting her with its nearness. His hands kneaded her thighs, push-

ing them with a rough and hungry passion that made
the stars go out.

"Please," she begged.

He looked up. "Do you want me to stop?"

She stretched her hands towards him, begging for
his embrace. She needed him against her breast now,
her arms around him, loving and holding.

His eyes closed slowly, like a cat's, and he bent his
head again.

This time her response was sudden and wild, shaking her like a tree in a whirlwind, drawing helpless
cries from her throat. Pleasure stormed through her,
leaving her alone and trembling.

"Jaf!" she cried on a high, yearning wail, and held
out her desperate arms. "Please, please love me!"

It struck him like a blow. He was helpless in the
face of such a cry. He tore and kicked off the sea-
soaked fabric that clung to his body, then, painted in
moonlight and shadow, lifted himself over her.

She moaned her wild expectation and lifted her hips
to meet the hungry, dangerous thrust of his. He pushed
his way home with a suddenness that rocketed sensation into every cell, drew away and pounded home
again.

The deeper pleasure that had teased and beckoned
hammered out of her blood with a wild, crashing,
blinding heat that robbed her of breath, of voice, of
sense.

She flew high, aware only of the distant thunder of
his body beating into hers, the high, melting heat and
light that was both the moon and not the moon, the
shivering surrender of her heart to a pure pleasure she
had never known existed.

"Jaf!" she cried, for that pleasure was freedom from fear. "Love me, Jaf, please love me!"

It fountained up in them, a mingled joy and torment, love and anguish, light and darkness, for opposites are the hallmark of the One. The stars burned into supernovas, blinding them both, and then winked out.

The sky was just beginning to lighten beyond the broad door that stood open onto the courtyard. Lisbet could see a white flower against the shadows.

Her body was both sore and languid with the memory of pleasure. He had pushed her, held her, made her muscles stretch and clench and then shiver into a thousand shards as joy rushed through her blood, again and again.

*Allahu akhbar. Allahu akhbar.*

In the distance the village muezzin was calling the faithful to prayer.

Her back was against Jaf's chest, and she could feel his heartbeat, strong and steady, through her system. He had burned his anger out at last, and sex had been the flame. She thought of the moment when, lying on the beach, she had felt the beat of love in her heart and understood, too late, what she had lost.

Thrown away, she amended. She had let fear rule her, and this was the result. So her heart told her.

Was it fear? her head replied. Or was it some deeper instinct that had known he would just repeat for her the experience of her father? In London she had seen no sign of his gambling, his profligacy. But perhaps the signs had been there for her unconscious to read.

Whatever the truth, she could not see the way forward from here. She loved him, now, when he no longer loved her.

And if she tried to win back Jaf's love, knowing what she now knew about him, she was a fool. A gambler was little better than a drunk.

No way was she going to marry her father.

She knew more about herself, too. When she had split up with Jaf, she saw now, she had been half hoping he would pursue her. She hadn't really wanted him to accept her decision.

She wasn't sure now what she had wanted to prove if he did come after her. But she had successfully hidden her disappointment from herself when he did not, and that had allowed her to come to the Barakat Emirates imagining she could meet him without risk.

Had she been lying to herself all the time?

As the honey of the night's lovemaking still flowed through her cells, sweetening every sense, Lisbet could see no way forward.

Slowly the light increased. The white rose revealed itself as pink, and the leaves behind turned from black to green. She lay without stirring, letting thoughts wander through her head, till the golden rays of sun streaking across the tiles of the courtyard told her it was past time to rouse herself.

Jaf's hand was locked on her hip, possessive even in sleep. Lisbet tried to slip away without disturbing him, but his arm unconsciously lifted to embrace her, drawing her back.

She turned her head to watch him in sleep. He was on his side, naked except for the sheet lightly draped over the prominent bone structure of his hip. The taut flesh fell away under the hipbone, creating a cave of shadow where his sex lay hidden.

He had a strong build, his upper body all muscles, neatly tucked and folded one into the other. His legs, too, she remembered from the night. He was a man at a peak of physical perfection, and his agile endurance had worn her out.

He had said he had nothing to offer her now but sexual pleasure. If there was ever a man who could make that addictive for her—she was looking at him.

An Olympic sportsman, too, she reminded herself, and with a sigh allowed herself to be drawn in against the warmth of his body. She was a fool, but...not yet, oh, not yet.

He awoke because his flesh was stirring into life. His mouth against her ear, he whispered, "Good morning," and his hand stroked down her arm from shoulder to elbow.

"Good morning," she responded with a slightly wary smile. "Sorry to disturb you so early, but I've got to get moving. I'm due on the set."

His eyes closed, he smiled and nodded, stroking her thigh with intoxicating firmness, as if to underline his ownership. "When?"

"About an hour," she murmured, stretching involuntarily as he continued to caress her still pleasure-swollen flesh. Foolish to think she could have sufficient control to resist his lovemaking when she was actually in his bed.

"We can take the horses. It's faster," he said, his hand sliding over her breast, down her abdomen, to the nest of hair below. Melted sugar flowed just under her skin in the wake of his touch, and then, anticipating, in advance of it.

"All right," she murmured, agreeing to the unspoken part of his proposition, and with rough precision, he drew her thigh up over his hip and threw off the sheet, opening her body and legs to his lazy exploration.

His hand moved to tempt the cluster of nerves lurking hungrily under the still-damp thicket. Lisbet grunted a little in surprise at the speed of her own arousal, arched her back, and sighed the suddenly peaking pleasure out through her toes.

The sight and sounds of her ready response aroused him, and he wrapped his arm under her back and rolled her over, drawing her up to kneel over his body, making her legs straddle his hips, her full, lush breasts catching an errant ray of sun. Then he lifted his flesh to hers and, with a sigh of deepest satisfaction, thrust home.

*Stay me with flagons, comfort me with apples: for I am sick of love.*

### Sheikh Jaf To Be In Movie

Sheikh Jaf's impromptu appearance in Masoud al Badi's new movie, now being filmed in the Barakati desert, will make the final cut, according to sources. Apparently the scene that was involuntarily filmed when Jafar al Hamzeh invaded the set and galloped off with Lisbet Raine, the film's star, is so hot the director wrote it into the film.

Jaf's house was quite a bit closer than Gazi's to the location, and almost at once they fell into a routine. The gold-plated limousine would pick her up at the end of the day's filming and take her back to Jaf's house, where she would bathe and refresh herself and then, usually, they made long, delicious love as the last rays of the sun were drawn down into the sea.

That was their quiet time. When they got up, it was

sometimes to a meal prepared for them in the house and served at the table in the courtyard. But more often than not, Jaf would want to eat out. And then, inevitably, the ''public'' Jaf would take over, and he would be anxious to hit the high spots.

They went to expensive places like the Sheikh Daud, now, where they were certain to be noticed by the clique of foreign journalists who hung out in one of the bars there.

It was very different from their time in London, where Jaf had always seemed to want her to himself, where it sometimes seemed they could have talked forever. But those lovers' conversations were a thing of the past.

And no matter how Lisbet tried to change events, they almost always wrapped up the night at the casino. And Jaf almost always lost.

The Shalimar Gardens was quiet, discreet and very expensive. It was intended for the amusement of the wealthiest foreign tourists only. The Barakat Emirates might have a secular government, but gambling was still severely restricted and frowned on in the country.

Barakatis were discouraged from going into the casinos, which made Jaf's appearance there that much more noteworthy. The fact that he was throwing away the fortune he had so recently inherited from his father was becoming household gossip.

Everyone disapproved, including Lisbet, but Jaf was deaf to disapproval.

''Jaf, it's so *boring!*'' Lisbet would complain. ''Whether you win or lose, where's the excitement? It's just standing around waiting for the ball to drop in the right hole. Why don't you take up golf? At least you have some control over the ball!''

"Come on, Lisbet," Jaf would cajole her. "It's my turn for a run of luck. Any day now."

Of course she could refuse to go with him. But she was sure he dropped more money if she wasn't with him. And, although she hated to admit it, she wanted to be with him, wherever he was.

It was her father all over again. Both men, Lisbet realized fairly soon, had collapsed under a blow of fate. The fact that her father had experienced sudden unexpected loss, and Jaf sudden expected gain, had not made any difference to their responses, though she knew who she respected more. Each of them had changed from being a useful human being to lying around doing nothing, fixated on a game over which they had no control, and drinking too much. Neither of them had even tried to make something better of the hand life had dealt them.

Worst of all, she found, was that her attempts to prevent Jaf's worst excesses were nothing more than fodder for a hungry media. Sheikh Jaf's "troubled affair" with the star of the first joint British-Barakati film was a hot item in the Sunday papers back home.

But she was foolish to worry so much about what was going to prove no more than a brief affair. If there was one thing that was now totally clear, it was that, whatever the media thought, Jaf had no serious, long-term intentions towards her. He never talked of the future now, never made demands, never used the word *love*.

It was just the perversity of life that she now yearned for him to do so. *Life is suffering*.

The only way Lisbet could cope was by ruthlessly reminding herself how impossible a long-term relationship would be with Jaf, and pretending that she wasn't falling daily more deeply in love with him.

# Eight

Meanwhile, the country was eagerly preparing for the first state visit by the newly crowned Sultan and Sultana of neighbouring Bagestan.

Bagestan was one of the country's nearest neighbours, and an old ally. It wasn't long since the citizens of the Barakat Emirates had watched enthralled as the ruthless and unpopular dictator, Ghasib, had finally been driven out of Bagestan and the sultanate restored in the shape of the old sultan's grandson. Scenes of the Bagestani people, first staging silent protests outside the palace, and later cheering deliriously as their new sultan rode through the streets, had played endlessly on Barakat television.

Everyone knew that the princes of the Barakat Emirates had done all they could to aid in the restoration. After all, the old sultan's three grandsons had all been Cup Companions in Barakat.

The Barakatis had been almost as thrilled by the restoration as the Bagestanis themselves. And now the sultan and sultana had chosen to make the Barakat Emirates the destination of their first official state visit, both in recognition of this help and support, and as a signal of the return to the old ties that had historically bound the two nations prior to Ghasib's coup.

Numerous events were scheduled, but the one everyone wanted an invitation for was the Royal Grand Reception being held by the three princes in the magnificent Queen Halimah Palace in Barakat al Barakat.

All the Cup Companions would be there, of course, including those of the sultan and sultana, as well as the titled, the successful, the movers and shakers of the country. In addition, from the census lists of every city, town and village in the country, names would be drawn at random, and the lucky ones would receive an invitation to attend as the representative of their area.

It was the occasion of the century. A once-in-a-lifetime experience of history in the making. People would talk about it to their grandchildren. There was practically no one in the country who wouldn't give up their hope of Heaven to attend.

One evening, Jaf surprised Lisbet by handing her a large, thick envelope addressed in Arabic.

She felt its importance in the weight of the beautiful linen paper, the lushly embossed crest on the back flap, and sat without opening it for a few breathless moments.

"What is that written on the front?" she pressed.

"My name, and yours. Open it."

"What is it?" Lisbet whispered, afraid to guess, when she had lifted the flap to reveal a thick, luscious, gold-embossed card with an ornately engraved seal stamped into red wax. The flowing Arabic calligraphy was a work of art in its own right.

Jaf smiled. "Our invitation to the Royal Grand Reception for the Sultan and Sultana of Bagestan. When Karim asked, I said you'd like to be included."

"Oh, Jaf!"

Lisbet felt as if she'd stepped into a dream. She gazed down at the invitation. She was even more thrilled than she would have imagined. The event to mark the culmination in freedom of thirty years of struggle by an oppressed people!

She had a more personal interest, too, as Jaf already knew. She had known Dana Morningstar as a fellow actress in London. How interesting to meet her now, as the Sultana of Bagestan!

"Thank you!" she breathed, even more moved because it would have been so easy for him to deny her this pleasure out of his anger. "And he agreed I could go, just like that?"

Jafar laughed. "In truth, it's more of a royal command than an invitation. The old forms still apply between monarch and Cup Companion, and that extends to consorts. If you decide you don't want to go now I'll—"

"Decide I don't want to go to the celebration of the century?" Lisbet laughed half-hysterically. "Oh, but—Jaf, everybody will be...what will I *wear?*" she cried.

He smiled, as if he had been waiting for just this question, and got to his feet. "Come," he said. "Let me show you."

He led her to the large, pleasant, book-filled room he used as an office. In the shadowed interior he pulled a book from a shelf, reached in to pull a latch, and drew a section of shelving open to reveal a door. Keying in a code, he pushed that open, too, while she watched.

A light came on automatically, and he gestured to Lisbet to enter.

It was a tiny, square room, lined with steel. A small baize-covered desk had stools on either side, and a lamp. There were several doors set into the steel walls.

"I think you know my grandfather was a collector," Jaf remarked, moving to one of the safe doors while Lisbet perched on one of the stools at his command. Her heart was beating with a sense of mystery and excitement.

"He had a particular fondness for the jewellery of the Jalal Period."

That was the name, Lisbet knew, given to the two or three centuries of extraordinary flowering in the fine arts named for the reign of the great King Jalal, grandson of Queen Halimah. Perhaps the most important piece of the period was the famous Cup of Happiness, now in the possession of Prince Omar of Central Barakat. She had seen a picture of that in the paper.

Drawing open a steel door, Jaf reached inside to lift out several velvet boxes and a small wooden chest and set them on the table.

"Some of these treasures have been in our family for many generations, but it was my grandfather who really expanded it into a collection. It was a passion he transferred to me. I loved to look at the collection even as a young child, and my grandfather taught me a great deal as I grew older.

"He knew that any hope for his collection lay with Gazi and me. At his death he left it in trust only to my father, and thereafter the collection was to be divided. He left to me the pieces that comprised the Jalal Collection, and the remainder to Gazi.

"My father was forced to keep the collection intact, but he cared little for it and added nothing to it during his lifetime. I hope to do more with it."

Standing over her, Jaf lifted one of the boxes, opened it, and placed it before her on the table.

Lisbet was prepared to be stunned, for anything beautiful in Barakat was always measured against the Jalal Period, but at the sight of what was lying on a bed of maroon velvet she felt the blood rush in her ears.

It was a single, massive emerald pendant, its deep, rich green intricately engraved, on a chain of the most delicately and precisely formed diamond, emerald and ruby florets.

Lisbet had never seen anything so beautiful in her life. The modern jewellery that Jaf had given her in London simply couldn't compare. The piece glowed with beauty and the rich lustre of age, and the workmanship was unbelievably intricate and delicate. The little florets were so perfectly shaped her heart melted at the sheer beauty.

"It was a Golden Age for such arts," Jaf murmured, setting the case to one side and opening another. "Craftsmen of this calibre no longer exist."

The next box revealed a worked gold pendant set with a large square central ruby, a surround of diamonds and emeralds, and a milky-white pearl drop pendant.

Lisbet suddenly thought of the pathetic "pearl" ring

she had hoped to fool him with, and almost laughed to think of her own stupidity. Trying to fool a man who had a collection of jewels like this!

She glanced up at him, her eyes laughing. "No wonder you threw my ring into the desert," she said.

He returned her look with one of dark intensity. "Not because the pearl was false," he reminded her.

As the next case was opened, her eye fell on a strand of polished emerald beads that was breathtaking in its simplicity. Lisbet caught her lip between her teeth and shook her head.

An intricately worked flower brooch composed of petals of ruby, emerald and diamond was next. A ring carved from a single piece of ruby, inlaid with gold and set with emeralds. Earrings, forehead ornaments, bracelets and armbands were laid before her till she was dazzled by the sparkle and drunk with their beauty.

"This piece is called the Concubine's Tears," Jaf told her softly, opening a box to reveal the last piece: a circular pendant composed of ranks of tiny, tear-shaped rubies fanning out from a central emerald, all inlaid in worked gold. An inner and an outer circlet of emeralds bordered them. A large teardrop emerald hung quivering below. The necklace was a narrow chain set with cabochon-cut rubies and emeralds.

"Like the Cup of Happiness, it is the work of King Jalal's great Parvani jeweller, Nazim Gohari."

They were by no means the showiest stones. But something in its very delicacy seemed to catch at her throat. "Oh, how beautiful!" Lisbet whispered inadequately. "I've never seen anything so lovely! I'm almost afraid to touch it."

He smiled down at her, not surprised that she should

have understood that this was the prize of the collection, in spite of having none of the showy stones that the other pieces boasted. Works by Nazim Gohari were rare outside of the palace treasuries of the three princes of the Barakat Emirates. A few were in museums.

"Why is it called the Concubine's Tears?" Lisbet asked, still gazing at the piece, and feeling that perhaps it was because the concubine in question had wept when she saw a thing of such beauty. The workmanship was unimaginably fine.

"The piece has a history. It was ordered by Jalal from Nazim Gohari for his favourite concubine, Kumar al Nahar," Jaf told her, while she lifted the piece this way and that in the light.

"Kumar al Nahar was a most beautiful woman, with amazing accomplishments for her young age. It was said she could sing, recite her own poetry, write a beautiful calligraphic hand, and play several instruments. She also regularly stumped the king with her philosophical arguments and deep knowledge of the Quran.

"It's said that while in the market on a shopping expedition with her women one day, the king's favourite went to the shop of a silk merchant. The merchant had with him his nephew, whom he was training up in the business.

"Kumar al Nahar and the young man fell instantly in love. She ordered some silks to be brought to the palace, and the young silk merchant duly arrived in the harem.

"The two embarked on an affair that was full of peril, for if the king found out he might have them both put to death. But they fell more and more deeply in love, so deeply that they took wild risks to be together, putting themselves at the mercy of those who might easily violate their confidence and bring doom on their heads.

"Rumours reached Jalal's ears, but he loved the concubine so much he preferred to give Kumar al Nahar the benefit of the doubt. And he chose that moment to show his favourite increased favour. He ordered for Kumar al Nahar bigger apartments, enlarging her entourage and increasing her household.

"Meanwhile, rumours began to circulate about the young merchant, and angry citizens stormed his uncle's shop, for fear of King Jalal's wrath. The young man was forced to flee the city suddenly, without being able to see his beloved one last time to say farewell.

"Kumar al Nahar received a hurried, desperate message from her lover wishing her goodbye forever, and was inconsolably grieved. When the king next requested a visit with her, she accepted and prepared for his coming, but with a heart weighed down with sorrow.

"When the king arrived, she sat by him while food was served to him and her singers and dancers performed for him, and did her best to hide her grief.

"The king presented the jewel to Kumar al Nahar, and when she looked on its perfect beauty, her heart was assailed with the memory of her perfect love and her terrible loss. She fell unconscious, alarming the king and all who saw her.

"When she recovered consciousness she began to weep uncontrollably, tearing her hair and calling to heaven in her grief. Then she swooned away again.

When they tried to revive her, it was discovered that she had died.

"A friend of her lover in the city sent a messenger to the young man to inform him of her death, but the messenger returned saying that the young man had also died, on the same day as his beloved."

Jaf stopped speaking, and there was silence in the little room.

"Such beauty should be shared with the world. It would please me to have you wear this jewel—or choose any of the others—to the reception for the sultan," Jaf said, as calmly as if he were offering her a drink.

Location shooting was finally completed, and the movie crew moved into newly built sound stages just outside the capital, Barakat al Barakat, for the interiors. Jaf and Lisbet began to spend their time at Gazi and Anna's house, because it was so close.

They were a close-knit family, Lisbet discovered. In spite of Jaf's bringing disrepute on the family name, Gazi spoke to him with respect, and he consulted him, and listened to his advice, as often as the reverse.

Gazi and Jaf had together supported their sister, Nadia, through a difficult divorce recently, and Nadia was now living in the house with her baby daughter, Safiyah, while she waited for her lover to come and claim them.

Ramiz Bahrami had been Nadia's first love, as Lisbet already knew, but their father had forced her into marriage with another man. After three brutally unhappy years, Nadia had met Ramiz again by chance, and the predictable had happened.

That had been difficult enough. But then Ramiz had

disappeared, leaving her pregnant and at the mercy of a suspicious husband. Nadia and her baby had only just managed to escape.

All this Lisbet had learned months ago, back in England, on the day she and Jaf had first met. She had been astonished, on her arrival in Bagestan, to learn that Nadia was still loyally waiting for her lover to return to her.

"Hasn't she learned her lesson?" Lisbet asked Jaf with a dry cynicism born of her own dilemma. He looked at her gravely.

"She trusts him because she loves him, Lisbet. Perhaps it is something you could learn from her."

She swallowed and bit back the truth. It would serve no purpose.

"Are you two going to get married this time?" Anna asked her one day. Nadia was in the pool with Safiyah. The baby's ecstatic screams as she splashed made a pleasant background to their conversation.

Her mouth firm, Lisbet shook her head. "Jaf doesn't love me, Anna. This is an interlude only."

Anna stared. "Did he tell you so?"

"Yes. And anyway, Anna, don't wish it on me. Jaf's a compulsive gambler."

"What if he reformed for your sake?" Anna pressed. She would love to have Lisbet married to Gazi's brother, but not at the cost of her happiness. It was a dilemma.

"He won't do it for my sake," Lisbet said, swallowing hard. "He's easy enough on the surface, but scratch Jaf and he's still very angry and unforgiving underneath. He says his love is dead and I believe him."

They sat in silence for a moment. "Oh, Lisbet," Anna said at last, and Lisbet bit her lip hard.

"Well, that's life, isn't it? I should be grateful, and one day, no doubt, I will be. Life with someone like Jaf would be no picnic."

That was what she said. But that wasn't how it felt. Picnic? Her heart was convinced life with him would be a perpetual banquet.

Physically, Jaf was the lover to die for. His body gave her a pleasure that every day seemed more melting, more overwhelming than the day before. In every physical cell she felt daily more alive.

But Lisbet's heart pined for the love that had once been hers. She missed the intermingling of their souls that had once occurred. In London she had accepted that part of their lovemaking without realizing what it meant.

She remembered nights in London, when, the limousine following at a discreet distance, they had taken long walks in the rain, beside the Thames. Then he had been the perfect lover, if she had not been too afraid to realize it.

In the darkness, their souls seemed to merge. Then she had felt, without allowing herself to form the words, that she had found the other half of herself.

Jaf had believed it. "I knew it the moment we met," he had told her one rare, crystal-clear night, when the stars had appeared. They had left the hotel and gone for a long walk through the park and then across Westminster Bridge. Traffic was light, and in the middle of the bridge they had paused to look out over the river and the city.

"Even before that, when we spoke on the phone, I

had a sense of something momentous happening. When I saw you, I knew. As if an angel came out of a cloud and spoke in my ear. *Here she is.*"

She could not speak when he talked like this.

"Look at the stars!" he had commanded her, and she couldn't disobey. "Here in London you do not see the stars as they really are. The lights of the city blind us to true light. In my house in the desert the stars show you what they really are. Sparks from God's presence.

"Each star is a reflection of the divine light, do you feel it?" Jaf demanded.

She bit her lip without speaking, wondering where this was leading.

"God is unknowable, and yet is in the world. The mystics say that God begins as perfect emptiness and radiates presence through many levels of being until the material level is arrived at. That is how everything in the world is said to be One.

"And it is there, where the material world manifests, that Being for the first time divides into masculine and feminine.

"The division, they say, causes a deep yearning in the soul's two halves. And that is what humans are searching for—to restore the Divine Soul to unity. We go through the world, yearning for the perfect fit that is our other half, so that in our being together, the Divine Soul is unified again."

He stopped and turned her to face him, his arms encircling her with the rough ownership that both thrilled and terrified her.

"Do you see the truth of it, Lisbet?" he demanded, gazing down into her starlit face with a passionate hunger that shook her.

"It sounds wonderful," she choked, her heart almost too full to speak, because in the face of such knowing how could she argue that the world was not God's habitat as much as the heavens?

"Yes," he told her urgently. "And you, Lisbet, you are my other half. You and I were one soul in that moment before Creation tore us apart. And now, *Alhamdolillah,* we have found each other."

When she looked back on such moments now, she could not understand herself. What had made her drive such love away? Who was the real wastrel—Jaf, who only threw away money? Or she herself, who had thrown away something infinitely more precious?

# Nine

-----

**A**t Lisbet's request, they went back one Saturday night to Umm Maryam's restaurant to be away from the prying eyes that now seemed to follow them whenever they appeared together in public. She was hoping that, for once, he would be happy with a quiet evening.

At the end of the meal they were alone in the little upper room. Jaf's arm was around her, holding her protectively into his shoulder, while he lazily ate with his other hand. They were sharing a single dessert composed largely of nuts, spices and honey, that was called Happiness in Arabic. Lisbet could believe it. In the main room musicians were playing a curious collection of zithers and strangely shaped guitars. In the little enclosure they were very private.

"Mmmm!" Lisbet exclaimed, taking a last mouthful of the heady but too-fattening mixture. "Diet tomorrow. This is impossible to resist."

Jaf slipped the tiny spoon into his mouth and ate another mouthful, turning the spoon over to catch every drop with his tongue. His eyes were half-lidded with sensual response as he licked an errant drop of spiced honey from his lower lip.

"It tastes like you," he murmured, close to her ear.

The honey in her stomach seemed to catch fire, and rush out through her blood and nerves to every part of her. "Jaf," she protested on a whisper. She had no control now over her response to him. He could melt her with a word, a look, the slightest caress.

His arm tightened around her, his hand clasped her hip with the urgent possessiveness that both thrilled and frightened her. One little part of her mind was always monitoring such moments, and whispering warnings. She could never be sure whether he still blamed her, as she blamed herself.

What if, when the time came, he refused to let her go? He was a man of influence here. Suppose he could prevent her leaving the country? There was a fierceness in him sometimes that made her wonder how safe she would be if Jaf were her enemy.

Then, as if the universe were laughing at her fear—or was it hope?—he let her go, drew his arm up and consulted the gold watch on his strong, dark wrist. "The night's still young. How about looking in at the Shalimar?"

Lisbet's heart plummeted. The look in his eyes now was the one she dreaded: rueful determination, as if he hated the compulsion that drew him there, but still gave in to it.

"No," she said quietly. "I don't want to go to the casino tonight, Jaf."

He nodded. "All right. Shall I drop you at Gazi's,

or would you rather stay at the house tonight? I can join you later wherever you are.''

''Jaf,'' she said, in a low, tormented voice.

''Lisbet, don't say it.''

*''Please,''* she begged, exactly as she had heard her mother plead, when her father was going to the pub. ''Please don't go.''

''I won't stay long,'' Jaf promised. As her father had promised.

She closed her eyes. But she was as helpless against the urge to plead with him as he was against the urge to go. ''Please stay with me, Jaf. Please don't go to the casino tonight.''

His eyes were black with an unreadable emotion. ''Not tonight,'' he said. ''Soon, Lisbet. This won't last forever.''

*Next time,* her father used to say. *Next time, I swear.* Or he would agree, take off his cap, and sink down in front of the television. But half an hour later he'd be gone. Nothing swayed him. Even when there was no money to buy food for his children, there was money for drink.

She looked at Jaf now, and wondered why it was that people are driven to repeat their worst life experiences, over and over. ''You're fooling yourself if you think you ever loved me,'' she said harshly.

A dark, almost frightening expression crossed his face. His jaw clenched so that the muscles bulged. He lifted a hand to stroke the hair from her cheek, tucking it behind her ear with a trembling restraint that made her eyes burn.

''I loved you more than you can dream of,'' he said roughly, his voice shaking. ''You are asking for something that I can't give you, Lisbet. Not now. Trust me. Why won't you trust me?''

"That's what my father said," she told him. "Every night. Sorry, but I used up all my blind, stupid trust before I was fifteen. You can call this whatever you like, Jaf—a passing phase, a mood—but please don't ask me to take you on trust while you continue in it. If you were really to be trusted, you would stop this insane compulsion now.''

He closed his eyes and breathed deep, letting her run to a standstill. Then he looked at her with dark, stern eyes.

"Lisbet, you are quick to judge. You question me and my motives so readily. Do you ever question yourself? Do you ever ask yourself whether it is right for you to lose all your ability to trust because of this experience with one man?''

"My father," she pointed out.

"Yes, he was your father! Even so, Lisbet. The universe is bigger than one man. You cannot throw away all your trust because one man was weak!''

"I'm not judging you by my father, though, am I? I'm judging you on your own actions. I'm making a decision based on my prior experience, I grant you. A man in the grip of an obsession isn't to be trusted, that's the plain and simple truth.''

Somehow she felt as if her words were the doom of their affair. She thought, *However long it takes me to finish it, this is when it ended.* Hot tears welled up. She bent her head, blinking them back.

"I was obsessed by you once, but no more," Jaf said harshly.

"I meant gambling.''

"That is nonsense! I am not addicted to anything.

I pay money to be entertained, as everyone does. I pay more for my entertainment than most people, that is all. I *have* more money than most people."

"Not for long, at this rate."

"So, it is because I might one day be poor that you feel as you do? You do not wish to share the bed of a lover who is a poor man? What excuse will you make for yourself when the next man comes along?

"It is too late for us, Lisbet, but if you do not work to free yourself of this fear, you face nothing but emptiness."

His words were broken glass scraping her heart. It was the first time he had said it. *Too late.*

"You're just trying to put me in the wrong!"

"And you are making up stories for yourself, so that you can run from life. It is an excuse! You look for excuses! You ran from me in London, and what was your excuse then? That I gambled? No, because you never once saw me gamble before you came here. What was your excuse then, Lisbet?"

She hated this. "You know what it was. And it wasn't an excuse."

"You tell me. Put it in words, Lisbet, if you can."

"You were being too possessive." She shifted uncomfortably, because she did not want to admit to him how much she regretted her actions. "You were trying to—own me."

"Own you!" he exploded. "I loved you. I wanted you to be my wife. I wanted to spend my life beside you. This is what the whole world does, Lisbet, if they are lucky enough to find the person they seek!"

"It wasn't something I ever wanted," she said stoically. "I made up my mind when I was fifteen that I'd never get married, never have children."

He shook his head. "At fifteen, a child's brain is not even fully developed, so it is not surprising that you made such a wrong and life-denying choice then. But are you going to base your whole life on a decision made by someone with so little experience of the world? One day, if you live, you will be eighty, Lisbet. What will that old woman think of the child's opinions of life?"

He was right, and perhaps she recognized it in some part of herself that was only just coming into awareness. But confrontation is not hospitable to subtle knowing, and besides, Lisbet was afraid to give away one of her supports out of fear of undermining the other. She was very sure of her ground there.

"Any woman of eighty would tell me I'm making a mistake getting involved with an inveterate gambler," she said, in a flat voice.

"You are talking like a fool."

Anger came to her rescue. "When I was a kid, there were times we went hungry because my father had taken the housekeeping money to buy beer. I'm not letting myself in for that again!"

Jaf laughed, a long, loud peal that, for a moment, stopped the conversation in the outer room of the restaurant.

"So that is your reason? You are afraid of going hungry? What about your own career, Lisbet? You are a professional, working woman. Can you not hope to feed yourself?"

"That's not what I mean, and you know it!" she cried furiously, because he was making her feel small and stupid. "Although let me point out that when my father had drunk his way through his dole money he quite often moved on to my mother's earnings.

"What I am talking about is the sense of betrayal I felt, knowing my father cared less about me than he did about his next pint of beer! A child is very capable of making those connections, you know. You can't protect yourself against loving your own father, you can't stop that hurting, no matter how often it happens."

He sobered suddenly, looking at her with an open, deep, understanding gaze. "Ah, I begin to see," he said, lifting a hand to stroke her hair back from her cheek. "Yes, now I understand you better. Lisbet, I am not your father. It is not as you think. If I could tell you—" he began, but Lisbet, terrified by the melting of her heart, shook her head so violently, her eyes squeezed shut, that he stopped.

"If you aren't an addict," she said, "it's simple enough. Don't go to the Shalimar tonight."

"Lisbet, is it beyond your comprehension that the world may not be exactly as you imagine it to be?"

"Otherwise, drop me at Gazi's, please."

Black flames burned up behind his eyes and she held her breath and sent up an urgent prayer that she would win.

"Fine," he said, pushed the table out, and got to his feet.

The next day the Sultan and Sultana of Bagestan arrived at Barakat al Barakat port in the magnificent royal yacht. The city was alight with happiness and goodwill. Cheers rang in their ears and streamers and fresh flowers poured out on their heads as the royal couple drove up from the docks to the Queen Halimah Palace, accompanied by the three princes of the Barakat Emirates and their wives, all in open cars, with thirty-six mounted Cup Companions as escort.

Everyone was crazy with delight at the pageantry. Something always came over the citizens of Barakat when all three of their princes appeared in public together, and this day the delirium hit an even higher pitch.

It wasn't merely that so many Barakatis had family connections in Bagestan that they took the restoration personally. People also instinctively felt that the restoration made their own monarchy more secure. President Ghasib had interfered in the affairs of Barakat for years before his downfall, secretly trying to destabilize the reign of the princes.

And even now there were dissidents and extremists who didn't know when they were well off. In addition to everything else, the fact that there was no Ghasib in the background, fuelling discontent and financing dissent, lifted a burden of fear from the country's heart.

So the Barakatis were almost as ecstatic as the Bagestanis over the restoration, and the fact that the sultan and sultana were young and magnificently handsome only added to the joy and the sense of rightness. It was a heady time. Sirens blared, flags waved, blossoms rained down on the royal couple's heads, and the cheering never stopped.

Anna and Lisbet dressed for that evening's glittering event in a kind of stunned disbelief. Who would have guessed, a year ago in London, that these two friends would be standing together in a place like this, getting ready to meet princes and sultans?

"Are you *sure* we're not dreaming?" Anna said

once. "Could it be that I'm actually still in that hospital in London, with a concussion and a bump on my head, imagining all this?"

"Probably. But then, where am I?" Lisbet pointed out. "*I* didn't have an accident. I got home safely that night."

"Are you sure? Can we be absolutely certain that a taxi didn't run us both down?"

Lisbet paused dramatically. "Now you mention it...no."

"Well, then, there's only one thing to do."

"Carry on enjoying ourselves till we wake up," Lisbet agreed.

They certainly weren't likely to have any rude awakenings tonight.

"Is that from the Jalal Collection?" Anna squealed in breathless admiration as Lisbet lifted her necklace from its velvet bed.

Of course she had chosen the Concubine's Tears.

"Isn't it wonderful? Jaf insisted. He said this was a once-in-a-lifetime occasion and if we couldn't take the risk, what was the point?"

"I guess the gambler mentality has its good side," Anna joked.

"It must be worth millions. I'm going to be terrified of losing it all night long."

When they had finished dressing, the two friends stood side by side in front of the mirror, gazing at themselves.

Their outfits, Anna's white and Lisbet's green, fitted with all the perfection that only hours of painstaking cutting and fitting on the part of a top dressmaker could achieve. Each wore a king's ransom against hair and skin that glowed almost as richly as the jewels themselves.

Anna's jewellery was a stunning sapphire-and-diamond set that Gazi had bought for her in London. In a creamy, sleeveless, calf-length tunic over the flowing Barakati pants called *shalwar,* with her black hair and dark blue eyes, and her warm golden skin, she was a vision.

To set off the magnificent ruby-and-emerald jewel at her throat, Lisbet wore emeralds at her ears, but nothing else was necessary. Her eyes, darkening to match, appeared to be two more precious jewels.

Her strapless silk dress, in a rich deep green to match the emeralds, clung to her body, the fabric drawn together at the hip. The skirt was slit on one side to reveal a matching gold-spangled panel of transparent georgette behind which the tanned skin of her leg was tantalizingly visible when she moved.

Around her shoulders she carried a stole of the same gauzy fabric, also spangled with gold.

Anna shook her head in admiration of her friend's green-on-green beauty.

"Look at you, Lisbet, you're way out of the ordinary," she breathed. "You've always been a beauty, but there's just something about you now. You have real charisma. And I don't believe Jaf doesn't still love you."

To her surprise, Lisbet's eyes clouded.

"What's wrong?"

"Nothing. Jaf went gambling again last night, that's all. But I already know he's not going to give it up, so if I'm disappointed, I'm a fool."

Last night she had locked the bedroom door against him for the first time in their relationship. It had taken her hours to fall asleep, but she hadn't heard him try her door in all that time.

"Did it make you happy, to sleep alone?" he had asked this morning, in a voice that made her skin twitch.

She had steeled her resolve. "I would have been alone most of the night anyway, wouldn't I? You must have had a very good night at the tables."

Immediately afterwards he had gone out on business with Gazi and the men had returned only in time to dress for the reception.

"I don't say you're not right, Lisbet, but you know, I asked Gazi about it, and he swears Jaf will be okay. He says there's absolutely no question he'll give up all his crazy ways if you give him time."

"How much time is he going to need, did Gazi mention?" Lisbet asked dryly.

"I know, I said that—why doesn't he just give it up now? And all Gazi could say was, he won't just yet."

A choke of mirthless laughter escaped Lisbet. "Men. What a club."

"I know it looks like that, but—I don't know, Lisbet. Could there be something going on we don't know about?"

Lisbet gave her friend a look. "Oh, sure. The instructions in his father's will mean he has to gamble away half his money in order to keep the rest?"

"Well, no, but…Gazi did once say that there would be things he couldn't tell me about. He said, *You need to know that I am a Cup Companion, and that there are some secrets not even a wife can be told.*"

"I'll just bet there are. And one of them is a secret family propensity for risk-taking."

Anna made a face. "I guess I'm being too far-fetched. And maybe Gazi is just saying that about Jaf to keep me from getting stressed just now."

Lisbet caught it immediately. "Why especially now?"

Anna smiled a slow, happy smile that spread all across her face. "I have to tell you first, Lisbet. I'm pregnant."

"Oh, *Anna!*" Lisbet embraced her friend with little thought for the perfection of their clothes and hair, smiling and exclaiming. "There couldn't be better news!"

A year ago Anna's life had seemed nothing but tragedy. What a transformation there had been.

Anna was blinking hard to protect her makeup from the happy tears. "Gazi's over the moon. So you see how much we'd both like it if you two could sort things out. Wouldn't it be lovely if our kids could grow up together?"

Lisbet was silent. The old, automatic rejection would not come to her lips. She looked at Anna's still-flat tummy and thought of the child growing there, and all she could feel was a pang of yearning.

All the old certainties were shifting. But to what benefit?

*It is too late for us, Lisbet.*

# Ten

The "pleasure gardens" of the Queen Halimah Palace were a masterpiece of architecture. They had appeared in several books and photographic studies, but no photograph could have prepared Lisbet for the staggering beauty she saw.

There were water steps and cascades, arches and pillars, fountains and pools, cloisters and colonnades, pavilions and pergolas, all in the most beautiful workmanship and materials—marble, sandstone, walnut, cedar, mirror and painted tile. There were citruses and plane trees and cypresses, roses and box hedges and pomegranates.

Everywhere she turned a new vista opened up, whether it was a double phalanx of cypress lining a water channel descending through several levels, a spread of lush tropical foliage, a row of scalloped arches, or a spacious, shaded cloister. It was completely magical.

And the assembled guests were every bit as breathtaking and beautiful. The Barakati world had pulled out all the stops. Not merely the jewellery, but the clothes, were the most luxurious possible: the traditional costumes of Parvan, Barakat and Bagestan were lushly embroidered tonight with gold and silver thread, mimicking the royal court of the Golden Age. The fabrics glowed in the flaming torches and lamps that illuminated the gardens as the sun set.

The food, too, was simply out of this world. There were skewers of delicately grilled chicken, salmon, or lamb, tiny pastry cups filled with delicious pastes of aubergine, tomato, peppers, onion, courgette and unknown others, intricately carved raw vegetable flowers, pastry envelopes wrapping a delicious mix of savoury herbs and cheese, tiny mounds of delicious bulgur-and-parsley salad on miniature lettuce leaves, toothpick kebabs comprising no more than a mouthful, balls of spiced minced lamb, mushrooms stuffed with rich, spicy cheese, vine leaves wrapped around savoury rice; the scent of cumin, coriander, cardamom, cinnamon.

Instead of wine, a fascinating variety of drinks was on offer—the date juice she had already learned to like, a light, tangy yogurt drink, a variety of delicious and unusual mixes of fruit juice.

And all in an endless procession, carried by beautifully costumed, dark-eyed children ranging in age from ten to about sixteen, all clearly proud of being chosen for this duty and on their mettle.

Groups of musicians playing every variety of Middle Eastern instrument were tucked into corners, under trees, by fountains, under cloisters, in pavilions. The music they played travelled hauntingly on the evening air, and as Lisbet and Jaf moved through the pleasure garden, they would lose the sound of one orchestra and a moment later come into range of another.

It was a night she would remember all her life.

Jaf wore the traditional ceremonial dress of the Cup Companions: the flowing white pants called *shalwar* worn under a richly coloured, high-necked silk jacket belted with a jewelled strap holding a glittering scabbard, and bedecked with a thick double rope of pearls thrown over one shoulder and caught high on the left breast with a fat jewelled pin. The Cup Companions could wear almost any colour of jacket. Tonight Jaf's jacket was indigo, and his eyes were black.

She had never seen him look so heartbreakingly handsome.

Jaf returned the compliment. When she and Anna had come down the beautiful old stone staircase to the terrace where the men were waiting, for a moment neither Jaf nor Gazi had spoken a word. But the expression in Jaf's eyes had been enough. And as he put an arm around her to shepherd her out to the car, she had felt him tremble.

The hostility of last night and this morning was forgotten, and now they stood together in the glory of the royal court and knew that, whatever happened between them, this night would never pass from their memory.

A young boy with a tray full of delectable tidbits paused by them. Jaf bent over the tray with frowning concentration.

"What do you recommend, Afif?" he asked the child in English.

Without hesitation, the child indicated the bowl on the right.

"Take the sall-mon, please, cousin," he said.

"The salmon?" Jaf obediently picked up one of the little sticks and popped it into his mouth. "Very tasty," he approved. "Is the other not so delicious? Nonetheless, it seems to have been eaten."

"It is not called *nonetheless,* it is called *breast of chicken,* and people like it so much that my tray has become unsteady. That is why I asked you to eat from the bowl on this side," the child informed him gravely.

They laughed and helped themselves to the little skewers of salmon, and the child nodded solemnly and moved on.

"Why did he call you *cousin?*" Lisbet asked, wondering if it were a translation of some kind of formal title used between children and adults.

"Because we are cousins," Jaf told her with a smile. He gestured with a hand. "All the children serving tonight are from the royal family or the families of the Cup Companions. It has always been thus."

"And will they grow up to be Cup Companions in their turn?"

"Some will, no doubt."

"Did you do it?"

"My grandfather was advisor to Sheikh Daud for many years. As a child, I served at many such occasions. But I do not remember one of such magnificence as this.

"One day, *insha'Allah,* my sons and daughters will serve in this way. It is an important training for those who are born to rank, to teach them that service is both a duty and a privilege."

Lisbet couldn't speak just at that moment, so filled was she with the ache of hopeless yearning. She had given up her chance to be a part of this. Anna's child, probably, would one day learn the simple truth about service in this way, but not her own child. She thought of Jaf as a father, holding his child close, and her heart clenched with yearning.

*It is too late for us, Lisbet.*

For perhaps the first time, she looked at the spectrum of human life and saw that it was a continuum, a passing on from one generation to the next—of duties, of wisdom, of information, of genes. Long ago, unhappiness had caused her to decide to isolate herself from the continuum, to have the thread of what she was stop with her. She had thought of childhood as too full of suffering to pass on to others.

But childhood was more than suffering, even her own. The bonds she shared with her brothers and sisters and her mother had supported them all through the hard times.

She was the one who had taken their father's downfall hardest. Lisbet now remembered, with a little shock, that as a young child she and her father had been very close. Perhaps because she had been his first daughter after two sons, she was closer to him than any of the others.

Had that made the betrayal that much harder to bear? That he would not give up drinking even for her? There was a host of memories in her mind suddenly, of moments when she had tried to use her power with her father to sway him from his chosen course. Like her mother, she had failed.

Looking back now, Lisbet could see that on each of those occasions her father had already been drunk. She had been pleading with beer, not Edward MacArthur. But how could a child have understood that? Even many adults could not distance themselves in such cases.

"What are you thinking about, Lisbet, that your eyes have gone so grave?" Jaf's voice softly broke into her musing.

She looked up into his eyes, her heart in turmoil. If she had given in to love when it was first offered, would she now have the power over him that she had never had over her father? Or would it be a repeat?

She would never know. *It is too late for us.*

Those words would drive her to an early grave, and then be written on it.

Gazi and Anna were coming along the torchlit marble path running beside the channel of flame-spangled water which led from a pool under a beautiful pavilion down to the fountain where the couple stood.

Jaf consulted his watch. "It is our moment to be presented to the sultan and sultana," he told her, as the other couple arrived.

Anna and Lisbet exchanged glances. However democratic your principles, there was still something that thrilled to the idea of meeting a sultan.

"Lisbet's met the sultana before, haven't you, Lisbet? In her previous incarnation as an actress in London," Anna said as the two couples moved off, arm in arm. Gazi turned a curious glance on Lisbet.

"Gazi wasn't there when you told me, remember?" Anna prompted.

"About three years ago we did *Midsummer Night's Dream* together in the Park," Lisbet explained to Gazi. "She played Helena and I was Hermia. We had a great time, but right afterwards I went on tour and we lost touch. I wonder if she'll remember me.''

They passed from the smaller side garden into the huge, brilliantly lighted square, bordered with trees, where the magnificent pillared pavilion stood. In front of it was a pool from which a fountain jetted up, the water catching the light from the thousand torches and multiplying it into a million shards.

The pavilion was reached by a short, broad flight of stairs. The four royal couples were standing at the top, and people were moving slowly up and down. Two ranks of men in the glittering ceremonial uniform of the Palace Guard lined the stairs looking very ornamental, but Jaf informed her in an undervoice that they were among the best trained bodyguards in the world.

"Those scimitars on their hips aren't merely ornamental, either, however jewelled the scabbards. Security here is a lot tighter than it looks."

Lisbet was startled. Security had looked pretty tight to her. Guests had passed into the palace only after a search by a handheld metal detector, which had reacted hysterically to every bit of metal anyone wore.

"Really? Why?"

"Because there are still some who would be very happy to cause the downfall of the princes of Barakat. Ghasib was not the only man in this region with an agenda. Look up there."

She followed the direction of his glance. Above them, on the roof of the pavilion, she could just make out several dark shapes.

"The secret service has mounted one of the biggest operations in its history to cover this event."

Jaf's office as Cup Companion, Lisbet knew, was the rough equivalent of a Minister for the Arts, with the particular focus of fostering cultural exchanges between West Barakat and the world. She wondered how he knew so much about the operation.

"Are you part of it?" she asked.

"All Cup Companions constantly take some part in the protection of the princes," he said. His hand unconsciously rested on the handle of his own gorgeously bejewelled sword.

"Is your sword real, too?"

He smiled. "It is the sword of my ancestors. Fine *jawhar* steel, still beautiful and deadly. You would call it *damascened.*"

They moved up the steps in the wake of Gazi and Anna then, in the flickering torchlight that lined both sides of the staircase. At the top the *talar,* or balcony, was bathed in a golden glow from a series of beautiful cut-crystal and bronze lamps.

Lisbet gazed up at the royal couples on the *talar* above her as she mounted the steps. It was a sight to take the breath away. She simply stopped breathing in the face of such beauty and majesty. However many photos one saw, nothing could equal seeing five ruling monarchs—for the sultana shared executive power with her husband—together in one place. The sense of real power was palpable and overwhelming.

They were all magnificently dressed in brilliant colours, gold, and jewels that sparkled richly in the golden light. They were all instantly recognizable to anyone who read the paper or watched television.

But recognizing them and meeting them in person were two very different things, Lisbet found, as she made her first curtsey and was presented to the prince to whom Jaf was most closely connected.

Prince Karim, dark and clean-shaven, wore a sapphire jewel on his turban and pearls over his shoulders. The Great Seal of Shakur, a magnificently carved emerald clasping his arm just above the elbow, glowed with green fire against his cloth-of-gold jacket.

There was no sign of his disapproval tonight, no distance between the prince and his erring Cup Companion, a fact Lisbet noted with relief.

Beside the prince, Princess Caroline was wearing an emerald in the middle of her forehead that made her beauty look other-worldly, but her smile seemed very real, and so did her interest in Lisbet and the film.

Next, Prince Rafi, dark and smiling, with a thick moustache, exuded warmth and charm. He wore a ruby in his turban, and at his hip carried the Sword of Rostam in its intricately jewelled ceremonial scabbard. Beside him, Princess Zara, her eyes glowing with warmth, wore white gold-embroidered silk with diamonds and rubies.

She, too, spoke to Lisbet about the film.

"We like to think Rose Dumont set up her headquarters in the ruins at Iskandiyar," she said. "We were hoping the film could be shot there, did you know? But it just wasn't possible to let it be used as a location at the moment, with the museum still being built."

"I'm very much looking forward to visiting Iskandiyar while I'm here," Lisbet responded.

"Well, Jaf must bring you. Jaf, do you hear that?" She reached out and put her hand on Jaf's sleeve. "Will you bring Miss Raine to the site sometime soon? Call first to let me know, so I can be sure to be there."

Prince Omar, tall and erect, with the neat pointed beard that was his trademark, wore in his ceremonial gold turban an emerald that matched his haughty green eyes. Prince Omar was intimidating, until his face softened when he looked at his pregnant wife.

Princess Jana, a warmly tanned redhead, was wearing a wonderful gold outfit that matched her husband's ceremonial jacket and turban, and glowed like one of the hanging gold lamps behind her head. Her neck was wrapped with half a dozen strands of the most luscious pearls Lisbet had ever clapped eyes on.

Then they were approaching the Sultan and Sultana of Bagestan. A voice announced, "His Excellency Jafar Zaki ibn Bassam al Hafez al Hamzeh, Miss Lisbet Raine," and Lisbet found herself looking up into the smiling eyes of a magnificent creature she could barely recognize as Dana Morningstar.

The sultana was wearing a breathtaking outfit of deep purple-and-turquoise silk and silk georgette, encrusted with gold embroidery and spangled over with gold diamanté and hundreds of minuscule gold mirrors. Nestling in her black hair was a circlet of gold and diamonds.

Beside her the sultan looked compellingly imperious and majestic in cloth of gold and a blinding array of pearls and emeralds.

"Lisbet!" the sultana cried with a smile, and bent forward to kiss her cheek. "I heard you were coming tonight. How wonderful to see you again! What's it like working with Masoud al Badi? I always wanted to work with him."

Lisbet grinned. "Very rigorous," she said, and Dana laughed. The two women chatted together for a moment almost as they would have, Lisbet reflected wildly, meeting in a rehearsal room in London.

Against this backdrop the conversation seemed utterly incongruous.

But the pressures of the occasion meant it had to be curtailed. "Ash," Dana murmured, leaning into the sultan's shoulder to interrupt his low-voiced conversation with Jaf, "Lisbet is an old friend."

As Sultan Ashraf Durran ibn Wafiq ibn Hafzuddin al Jawadi Bagestani's imperious dark eyes fell on her, Lisbet's curtsey was completely instinctive.

"Your Majesty," she murmured. No wonder the Bagestanis had wanted the man as their sultan! No wonder they had risked life and freedom, taking to the streets to demand his homecoming.

He said something, and Lisbet replied without knowing what either of them was saying.

Then Dana said, "Lisbet, every minute of our schedule is full while we're here. But when you've finished on the film, or if you get a break, will you come to Bagestan and stay with us for a few days? I'd love to really talk!"

"Good evening, Miss Raine," said a voice, and Lisbet turned to see a white-haired stranger in formal court dress standing beside her. She hadn't seen him before, but he was clearly a man of importance. He carried himself like a man used to power.

After their presentation, the foursome had strolled into one of the smaller pavilions on the grounds, where Lisbet and Anna had been enthralled by the architecture, paintings and furnishings.

Built on a square, with a ceiling of intersecting, descending domes, the main room of the pavilion was divided by a double circle of marble pillars that held up the pattern of domes.

A myriad exquisite Parvani and Persian carpets, all hand knotted in silk or fine wool, flung as if at random over each other, covered every square inch of the marble floor. More carpets hung from the walls, alongside silver-and gold-embroidered silk tapestries that glittered and glowed in the warm light of a thousand crystal lamps.

In every corner was the green of tall, leafy plants and trees. Here and there fountains played.

The guests relaxed on cushions and divans as richly coloured and embroidered as the hangings and the carpets, while the endless supply of tidbits borne by the children continued.

Stationed at one corner of the room, a small orchestra playing traditional instruments provided a haunting background to the buzz of conversation.

Jaf's attention had been caught by someone, and Lisbet had wandered out of the main room into a smaller area, examining the paintings and hangings.

Now she was standing in front of a portrait of King Daud, the princes' father. She looked up as her name was spoken. She and the stranger were alone in the small hall.

"Hello," she said, arching her eyebrows enquiringly.

But he did not introduce himself. "You are interested in our late king?"

"He had a very dramatic life, didn't he?"

"Ah yes. He, too, loved a foreign woman."

"Like his sons."

"Not only his sons. Are not you loved in this way?"

He smiled, but she was not fooled. Malevolence exuded from him like an acid mist, little drops that burned wherever they touched her, parching her lungs when she breathed. Lisbet would have liked to walk away. But something held her there. Perhaps his very malevolence.

"Do you think so?"

His eyes fell on her necklace. "Even a man as foolish as Jafar al Hamzeh does not allow any ordinary woman to wear the Concubine's Tears. Do you know the value of what you wear around your neck?"

She was conceiving a powerful dislike of this man.

"On the other hand, maybe he wanted it seen tonight. Maybe I was just the handiest neck."

He stared at her for a long moment, then nodded.

"You are a wise woman," he said, in carefully modulated admiration. "You understand that Jafar al Hamzeh is a poor risk. Gambling, drinking—how can such a man be counted on? We hear that you try to turn him away from the evil."

"Is that what you hear?"

"Forgive me if I take the privilege of my white hairs to tell you, Miss Raine, that if it is his rehabilitation you desire, you go the wrong way about it. A man like Jafar al Hamzeh will not be induced to stop gambling because a woman—however pretty she is— asks him. It is a sickness. There is only one cure for such a disease."

"And what would it be?"

He smiled and tapped the air with a forefinger. "Did I not say you were a wise woman? So many young people fail to understand how much grief would be saved if they would listen to the advice of their elders. It is a modern epidemic. But you understand."

The forefinger moved again. "The only way to treat this foul disease is to let it run its course. Turn your energies in the opposite direction, Miss Raine. Only when Jafar al Hamzeh has utterly wasted his inheritance and ruined himself can he begin to live his life as a sober, sensible man.''

She didn't waste her time getting indignant.

''I have seen it many times. The efforts of mothers, even, fall on desert ground with such men. Only the delivery of a deep shock allows such behaviour to change. Even Western psychiatrists are now learning this wisdom. You can help.''

Behind her the music floating from the main room added its own thread to this surreal scene.

''But if I encourage Jaf to gamble away everything, where will that leave me?'' she pointed out in gentle mockery. ''The deep shock may also allow him to reject me for my betrayal.''

''Ah, but you will recover, you will move on! I understand you and the business you are in.'' His voice dripped with unconscious contempt. ''Such as you do not expect to choose a partner for life, isn't it? A new movie, another leading man. It would be too much to expect more from such a lifestyle.''

With a little shock Lisbet understood that this was not an idle conversation. She also saw, with a clarity that frightened her, that here was a man with an agenda.

''In that case, why should I care what he does?'' she said, racking her brains for some clue as to what he could want. ''Should I bother trying to reform him if there is no long-term benefit to me?''

A look of quickly suppressed triumph crossed his face. He laughed admiringly.

''Very true. But consider, Miss Raine—if Jafar al Hamzeh faced his ruined life, took stock, and returned to the straight path to live as Allah intended, how his friends would rejoice! They would be very grateful to the one who had made him see the error of his ways. You need have no fear of losing anything by this course, I assure you.''

''I see,'' she said. ''That would make all the difference, of course.''

He nodded, completely missing the irony. He looked at her for a long moment, and then, as if they had understood something, took out a slim wallet, extracted a tiny gold pen, wrote a number on a card.

''You will know better than any other at what moment the shock has been delivered. On that day, call that number. You will not be sorry.''

Her eyes still on his face, Lisbet lifted her hand automatically and accepted the card.

*You're wrong,* she mentally told the man. *I'm not nearly as smart as you think. It's taken me all this time to realize that you aren't my enemy, but Jaf's.*

# Eleven

Lisbet tossed and turned till the sun came up. Only when the room was light did she finally fall into a fitful sleep, and when she awoke a few hours later, Jaf was gone.

She got up and staggered to the bathroom, where she stood for five minutes in a cold shower. *Nice to have been to such a blowout and not have a headache afterwards,* she thought absently. *There's something to be said for not having wine shoved at you at every turn.*

The only headache she had was from the blast of malevolence she had absorbed from the stranger. In retrospect, Lisbet shuddered. How could she have stood beside the man for as long as she did? She had dreamed of him as some kind of alien, nasty and sinister, with yellow eyes.

He seemed to her the kind of man who never gave

up, who would go on and on, a step at a time, till he got what he wanted. The fact that she refused to help him would disconcert him not a bit, she was sure. He would just wait for another opportunity.

And it was Jaf he was after. He wanted Jaf's ruin. The thought of such a man being bent on such a mission terrified her. Like a vulture, hovering, waiting, till his victim was too weak to resist.

And that was only half of what had kept her awake by Jaf's side last night. The other half was finally facing how deeply entangled she was. The nameless threat from the stranger had caused things to crystallize.

She loved him, deeply and completely. It would be like tearing her hair out by the roots to leave him.

For the first time, Lisbet understood that her mother had been half complicit in the pregnancy that had scuttled her chances of a different future. There had been a part of her that wanted to stay with her lover.

And for the first time she could see that, however hard life became, what had held her parents together was love. It was like looking at one of those graphics where dark and light markings seem meaningless, but if you look long enough an image suddenly appears.

And she must always have known it, unconsciously. The reason she had been so terrified of Jaf owning her was that she loved him. She had learned the lesson of her mother's life unconsciously, and it had guided her actions without her being in touch with her motives.

It was herself she was afraid of. Herself, and love.

And, she reminded herself, the man who had offered her a bribe to bring about Jaf's downfall.

It was late when she got down to the terrace, where everyone usually ate breakfast. Gazi and Jaf, she learned from the maid who refreshed the coffeepot, had gone out on business. Anna was in her studio, working. Nadia had taken the baby into town.

Lisbet waived breakfast out of deference to last night's gorging, and took a quick swim in the pool. With perfect timing, there was a delay in filming just now, while one of the harem sets was being rebuilt. There would be no filming for at least a week.

Thank God, Lisbet thought. She would have had a hard time concentrating today. But she pulled out her script and settled to trying to work on her lines for the scenes to be shot as soon as filming resumed.

Her attention wouldn't fix on Rose Dumont. Again and again she found herself mulling over the events and discoveries of last night. Strange how something so magnificent as the reception could be so overshadowed by a two-minute conversation. Strange how blank her mind was whenever she tried to think of the future.

"Are you ready for a drink of something?" Anna's voice broke into her thoughts after a couple of fruitless hours, and Lisbet turned gratefully to see her friend striding across the terrace to where she sat.

Anna was wearing a blush-pink swimsuit, her white terry robe flapping on the breeze. She was warmly tanned, her skin glowed and Lisbet couldn't help comparing this happy vision to the woman she had been a year ago. Then she had been too thin, depressed and listless, grieving over the man who had walked out on her and the stillbirth of her child.

Now her manner said she had everything to look forward to. Anna had never seemed happier. If only the same road to happiness were open to Lisbet.

She supposed it was just typical of anyone with a damaged childhood that she had somehow managed to repeat her mother's experience. Falling for an addict. If she did have children with Jaf, she would be giving them the same childhood that she had suffered through—the kind of responsibility-laden time that wasn't childhood at all. Always nervous about what Daddy was going to do. Trying to stop him from indulging in his addiction because it hurt everyone so much....

No, on the day she discovered she was pregnant with Jaf's child, if she ever did, she wouldn't feel the unalloyed joy that Anna clearly felt. For her there would always be mixed emotions. Her happiness would always have echoes of guilt and foreboding.

And if, as seemed more likely, Jaf never loved her again, how long would she grieve? Would she ever love another man the way she had finally realized she loved him?

Anna was carrying a big pitcher filled with creamy-white liquid, and two glasses, which she set down on the little table at Lisbet's elbow.

"This kind of thing drives the staff crazy," she confided with a grin. "But I think if you let yourself be waited on *all* the time, you get soggy. Okay if you're born to it. Piña colada, your favourite."

"Mmmm."

Anna filled the glasses and sat down. A tendril of yellow blossom from the wall stretched towards her in the breeze, and she caught it in one hand and brought it against her cheek, sniffing the perfume.

"Isn't this terrace heaven? Even on a boiling hot day like today, it's pleasant here. Is Jaf's place nice? I've never been there."

They chatted about houses, but the topic foremost in both their minds was last night, and it wasn't long before they were discussing it.

Lisbet managed to forget her worries in the excited postmortem of the evening.

"Well, we've gossiped over lots of parties on lots of mornings after in our day," Anna observed, after the subject had been thoroughly washed, wrung out and hung to dry. "But I think today we've peaked."

"You're right. It really was the party to end all parties. When we're sitting in our 'sheltered accommodation,' Anna—"

"Side by side in our comfort shoes and our E-Z loungers—"

"Complaining that no one makes piña colada the way they used to—"

"They will say of us—"

"*This* was our finest hour!"

Something else she would remember about the past twenty-four hours, Lisbet thought. She drained her glass of the deliciously sweet piña colada and set it down, suddenly grave.

"Something happened last night, Anna."

"Jaf proposed!" Anna cried.

"Nothing like that. It was quite frightening, actually." Lisbet embarked on the brief narration of her conversation with the stranger. When she had finished, Anna sat frowning and gnawing her lip.

"What did you make of it?" she finally asked.

Lisbet breathed deep. "I've been trying to work out what he really wanted. I keep thinking of the way he commented on the necklace. Do you think it could be something to do with the Jalal Collection? That would be a reason for wanting Jaf's financial ruin, wouldn't it? He might assume that Jaf would have to sell the collection cheaply if he lost big at the casino.''

Anna shrugged. ''Maybe. But I think Gazi would buy the collection if it came to that. Jaf has talked about giving it to a museum, and that would be okay with Gazi, but sell it to a private collector? I don't think either of them would like that.''

''The man who talked to me may not know that.''

''True…'' Lisbet could see that Anna wasn't convinced but couldn't find any concrete objection. ''One thing mystifies me—why this man assumed you would agree to do it.''

''I think it was just contempt. I'm a Western woman, I'm an actress, I'm sleeping with Jaf without being married—doesn't it follow that I'm totally corruptible?''

''Mmmm. But it's also possible, isn't it, that he's trying to spook Jaf?''

''You mean, said what he said hoping I would pass on his comments to Jaf?''

''*Have* you told him?''

''He was gone when I woke up.''

''Gazi, too. They both have a lot to do with the royal visit,'' Anna said. ''But they'll be back for lunch. Are you going to tell him?''

Lisbet looked out over the turquoise expanse of the sea. The heat was intense today, but the breeze was pleasant, as Anna said. A huge cruise vessel was sailing past. ''I'm almost afraid to. Do you think I should?''

Anna sat in silence for a moment, tapping a finger against her lips.

Lisbet recognized the signs and was silent, letting her think.

"Last winter, when it was all happening with Nadia—Gazi told me something. I can't tell you any details. But I have a feeling you should tell Jaf about this immediately. It may have much broader implications than appear on the surface."

"Where did you think you had seen him earlier?" Jaf asked.

"Jaf, there were so many people!" Lisbet protested. "When he spoke to me, I had the feeling I'd seen him before, that's all. I can't be certain."

"But not spoken to him? You hadn't been introduced at any point?"

"No. I'd remember that voice."

"You said you felt he was someone important," Gazi said. "Can you say why?"

She closed her eyes, trying to visualize the scene and her first reactions to the man. They waited in silence.

"At first I thought it was just because he had an aura of power," Lisbet said. "But I think maybe there was something else, too, something I'd seen earlier—maybe one of the princes talking to him in a certain way? I have the vague recollection of seeing something like that without really noticing it."

She had told Jaf about the meeting when the men came home for lunch. Jaf's reaction was convulsive. He had questioned her briefly and urgently, and then called Gazi. Now Lisbet and the al Hamzeh brothers were in Gazi's office going over the incident in minute detail.

"How sure are you that he didn't come into the pavilion after your conversation with him?"

"I'm almost certain he wasn't in the main room. I

was looking around for him because I wanted to point him out to Jaf.''

Gazi tapped the white card with the phone number against his thumb. "Is there anything else at all you can remember, Lisbet? Any clue?''

"I really think I've told you everything." She had been racking her memory for every detail of the man's appearance for the past half hour. "Jaf, can't you tell me what this is about?''

It seemed that Anna's suspicions were on target. The way Jaf and Gazi were reacting told her there was more than petty malice against Jaf involved. They were like wild animals, every sense alert at the approach of an enemy. Then she mentally amended that. Their attitude wasn't that of victims, but hunters. They were lions who had scented their prey.

"I am not sure how much we can tell you at the moment, Lisbet," Jaf said. "We will have to consult, and get permission before telling you anything.''

She blinked. "Permission?" She had never heard of Jaf asking anyone's permission to do anything. Except one. "Do you mean you have to talk to *Prince Karim* about this?''

The brothers exchanged glances. Gazi grinned. "And all this time I thought you chose her for her looks.''

Jaf's eyes rested on her with a look that made her heart skip. "I chose Lisbet for her soul," he said.

How could one heart be made both lighter and heavier by the same remark?

"Lisbet, we have to swear you to secrecy," Jaf told her that evening. The three of them were in Gazi's office again, looking out over a shaded nook of the terrace.

"It's a question of national security and I have to ask for your word not to speak of it. Anna and Nadia know some of it, but it would be dangerous to talk where you might be overheard. Do you agree?"

There was a kind of thunder in her ears. "You want to tell me national security secrets?" she breathed.

The men nodded, and she looked from one to the other.

"Why?"

Again the brothers exchanged significant glances, and Gazi clicked his tongue admiringly at his brother.

"You want me to do something," she said. "That's the only reason I can see for my needing to know anything."

"We want you to help smoke this man out of hiding," Jaf said. "You are the only one who has seen him, Lisbet. We think you've talked to the man at the top, or very close to the top."

Her heart was pounding hard. "The top of what, exactly?"

"Of an ongoing conspiracy to topple the monarchy of the Barakat Emirates."

"Oh, God!" she cried. "And how could I help?"

"By leading me along the road to ruin and then calling the number he gave you and demanding your reward," Jaf told her simply.

"As far as we know it started about twenty-five years ago," Jaf told her later, as they walked along the beach under the stars. "When a beautiful young woman appeared at the palace demanding to speak to the king. No doubt she had been raised on stories of the old courts, where the king held regular days of justice at which ordinary citizens could speak. Her name was Nusaybah. Perhaps you know the story of Prince Jalal.''

Lisbet nodded. She had read the story in a magazine at the time his identity was discovered. Jalal was the posthumous son of Prince Aziz al Quraishi who, with his brother the Crown Prince, had died in an accident before he could marry Jalal's mother. Only the king had known of his grandson's existence, but although he had educated the boy at great expense, he had left absolutely no provision for him on his death, hadn't even revealed his existence to the three sons—the present princes—to whom he left his kingdom.

Jalal had gone into the desert with his followers and become a bandit, demanding territory of the princes, thinking that they knew who he was. Only when, in desperation to be heard, he had taken Princess Zara—then Zara Blake—hostage, was the truth revealed.

''Yes, that is the story the public believes,'' Jaf told Lisbet now, as the soft sound of waves tumbled up the shore. ''But it is not the full truth. Last year Jalal was confronted by men who told him that the old king, his grandfather, had never known of his existence. Someone who was deeply opposed to the Quraishis, someone within the palace, had seen in Aziz's unknown young son a future weapon against the ruling family.

''It was this man who had taken charge of Jalal's education, who had seen to it that the princes never knew who he was, who had caused him to be spurned and become disaffected. The plan was to overthrow the princes and install Jalal as a puppet. But when the plan was revealed to him Jalal would have no part of it.''

Lisbet's mouth opened in a gasp of comprehension. "Is *that* why Jalal gave up his titles and left the country? I thought he renounced it all for love."

Jaf smiled, his face reflected in moonlight. "Love formed a part of his decision. But Prince Jalal was also determined not to spend his life, as he put it, 'a focus for every sect that is disenchanted with the state of the country.'

"Those who had invested so much in Prince Jalal have not given up on their dreams of power simply because no puppet prince is now available, however. They are looking for other means to achieve their ends."

Lisbet nodded. "Like what?"

"At the moment, we have learned, they plan to subvert one of the Cup Companions. We do not know exactly for what purpose at the moment."

"How have you learned that?"

"Ramiz Bahrami is undercover with this group."

"Ramiz! Is that—do you mean Nadia's…"

"That is why Nadia waits so patiently for him," Jaf said softly. "She knows that a higher duty makes its demands on him."

"Ohhhh."

His eyes watched her gravely in the starlit darkness. "I, too, Lisbet."

"You? You're working on this?"

"I am deeply involved with the attempt to expose these people before they can achieve their ends."

Her lips were dry. She licked them. He was trying to tell her something. What was he really saying here? A bird cried from the trees in sudden, sharp alarm. Shivers of unnamed dread started along her skin.

"And does all this have something to do with that man who talked to me last night?"

"We hope so. We think so."

"What is your involvement, Jaf?"

"I am proving myself a worthy target for subversion. A man who is in the grip of a passion like gambling may be a man whose loyalty can be purchased."

# Twelve

Lisbet closed her eyes as a dozen tiny clues clicked into place. The ridiculous, gold-trimmed car that did not seem like the Jaf she knew. The reluctant determination to go to the casino. The crazy way he bet.

"It was all a setup," she breathed. "It's nothing but a front."

He was listening closely for her reaction. "It is."

"Oh, God, and I fell for it! What a *fool* I am! That Rolls…" She closed her eyes, shaking her head. Opened them. The nervous bird shrieked out again.

"And all the money you're losing at the tables—where does that come from?"

"Prince Karim restores my losses. The Shalimar Gardens is a Crown property."

They walked in silence, their feet pressing white shapes into the dark sand, while she absorbed it.

"I really should have guessed, shouldn't I?"

His mouth was just slightly twisted. Bitterness, perhaps.

"But then, trust is not your strong suit," he said.

The words flicked her painfully. "Admit that your disguise is very good!" she cried indignantly. "You were in the papers for months with your extravagance and your lifestyle."

"You had known me for months before that, Lisbet. You chose to ignore your personal experience of me in private to accept the public face I was presenting. Isn't it so?"

"Not until I got out here and saw it for myself," she protested hotly. "Did you expect me to ignore the evidence of my own eyes?"

"I asked you to trust me."

"And *I* asked *you* not to gamble!"

"I told you I would give it up soon."

And suddenly there they were again, arguing.

"Oh, right! That and a bus pass will get you to Hammersmith! Everybody in the world is going to give up something soon!"

"Except you, Lisbet. You are not going to give up mistrust, are you? How can you blame me now, when you have been told—"

"Me blame you? It's you who are blaming me! All I said—"

He caught her shoulders. "There is no time for this luxury, arguing. We must know if you will help us."

"Of course I'll help you!" Lisbet snapped. "If you knew me as well as you think I should have known you, you'd know that!"

He gritted his teeth to contain his retort. "Then let us begin."

* * *

For the next week Lisbet lived the wild life of a rich man's pampered mistress. Jaf took her on wildly extravagant shopping sprees, ostentatiously buying her jewellery and clothes, brought a top London hair stylist in on a flying trip at enormous expense to do her hair, took her yachting, even ordered her her own monogrammed Rolls.

That was during the day. At night, inevitably, they wound up at the Shalimar Gardens, where Lisbet encouraged Jaf to gamble on her wildest hunches.

Pictures were taken of them, whatever they did. The papers loved this new twist of events, and everyone they talked to had a story to sell. Staff at the casino were interviewed and talked about the amount of champagne they consumed, the wild betting, how Sheikh Jafar seemed to be completely taken with the beautiful English actress.

Of course the journalists discovered that they had begun this affair long ago in London and that Lisbet had been the one to break it off. They printed every detail of the relationship they could dig up, and then some, including the fabulous flat in Primrose Hill.

The stories printed grew wilder and wilder. One said that the couple made love with Lisbet wearing jewellery from the fabulous Jalal Collection. Another suggested that Jaf had financed the film on condition that Masoud al Badi cast Lisbet in the lead, on purpose to bring her to the Barakat Emirates where he could woo her again. One even said the model for the gold statuette on the Rolls had been Lisbet herself.

In the King's Pavilion, seven men sat on cushions around the plashing fountains whose noise would hinder any attempt to eavesdrop on their conversation. Three of the men were the Princes of the Barakat Emirates—Omar, Rafi, and Karim. Three more were their Cup Companions, Hashem al Makin, Arif al Rashid, Jafar al Hamzeh. The last man, older than the others, was the Grand Vizier, Naseh al Rajulu Daulati.

"So we have him," Omar was saying.

"It is far from certain," Hashem al Makin informed them. "I will remind you all that we've had to carry out any investigations with the utmost caution, for fear of tipping off some unknown member of the conspiracy.

"Having said that, the phone number given to Lisbet Raine is a mobile phone registered to a woman named Rima Bokhari. She lives in al Fakri area."

"Al Fakri! And she has a mobile phone?" exclaimed Rafi.

"Exactly. However, enquiries uncovered the fact that the woman has a widowed daughter, named Afra al Haziya. This latter woman is rumoured in her own neighbourhood—which is somewhat more upmarket than her mother's—to be the mistress of a government official.

"Surveillance presented huge problems, since anyone of whose loyalty we could be completely certain would probably be known by sight to the target. With more time, we could, of course, be more certain. However, two sightings have been made in the neighbourhood. It is enough of a coincidence to be noteworthy at the very least."

"Who was it?"

The Cup Companion paused with unconscious dramatic instinct to glance at his audience. "Yadeth al Najaz."

The name fell among them like a brick through a

window. The six listeners took in one collective breath, and the splash of the fountain grew sharply loud, as if their silence had become somehow more complete.

"How certain is this?" Karim was the first to speak.

"Not certain at all, Lord. He was seen in the street behind this woman's house. There is a back door to the garden in that street."

"There's never been a whisper about Yadeth al Najaz's loyalty," Rafi said. "He's been around as long as I can remember."

"He became Father's Cup Companion before we were born, didn't he?" Omar mused. He turned to the Grand Vizier. "What can you tell us about him, Khwaja?"

The older man sat for a moment, marshalling his thoughts.

"Yadeth al Najaz must by now be nearly seventy years old. As you know, he is of the Najazi tribe, hereditary enemies of the Quraishi. Forty years ago, the climate among the tribes was much more volatile than it is today, and the Najazi were the ringleaders.

"Yadeth al Najaz was very highly placed within the tribe. I believe it was on the advice of Nizam al Mulk, my predecessor, that your father appointed him Cup Companion. Several other appointments were made at that time, in the effort to calm the hostility of the Najazi and convince them that there was no room for tribal hatred within a modern state.

"I always suspected that Nizam al Mulk was not entirely sanguine about the experiment. He advised your father never to put any of the Najazi men into positions of real influence or give them his deep confidence.

"That is why Yadeth al Najaz was appointed to palace administration—a nonpolitical role. He became Chief of Staff of all the palaces on the death of Mustafa al Nabih and served in that position until the death of your honoured father. And after your succession, of course, he was made *Sadin al Qasr* of Queen Halimah Palace."

The Queen Halimah Palace was the seat of the Barakat Emirates' joint government.

Omar stroked his neatly pointed beard. "Well, he would certainly have been in the right place at the right time. When Jalal's mother came to the palace demanding to see the king, it is very likely that he would have been called. And who better than he to intercept the mail thereafter?"

"The *Sadin al Qasr* also had full access to palace letterhead."

"And he had a ready-made grudge," added Karim. "Motive, means, and opportunity, all staring at us."

"Has Miss Raine had an opportunity to identify him?" asked Omar.

"One of the strangest coincidences is the lack of any photograph of Yadeth al Najaz over the past forty years," said Jaf. "We're trying to take a photograph covertly. Meanwhile, Lisbet has seen an old photo and certainly doesn't rule him out."

"Well, I think we can take it as a working hypothesis that we've found our man," said Omar.

"What was his original motive for not relaying the news of Jalal's existence to Father, I wonder?" Rafi mused. "He can't have conceived of the whole scenario at once. It must have grown over time."

"Think of the joy your father and Queen Azizah would have felt, if they had discovered that, against all the odds, they had a grandson," Jafar al Hamzeh suggested. "It may be that it began in no more than simple malice."

Karim nodded. "And perhaps a gut feeling that the boy could be used somehow, sooner or later."

"Well, it's time his career was stopped," Prince Omar said, with steely precision. He turned to Jaf. "You and the admirable Miss Raine seem to be doing a first-class job with the bait. Could you spring the trap anytime soon?"

"Now's as good a time as any," said Jaf.

On the evening of the day chosen for the final act of their drama, Jaf and Lisbet lay in the tangled sheets of his bedroom at Gazi's house, looking out over the bay. They had made love with a passion that took added urgency from the approach of danger. Now they talked calmly about what they were about to do.

"Tribal rivalry?" Lisbet repeated in astonishment.

Jaf nodded. "It's the only thing that makes sense. The Najazi-Quraishi feud has been going on for centuries. Only a Najazi would be capable of planning something against the royal house that was going to take a quarter of a century to come to fruition.

"And by the same token, when Jalal destroyed Yadeth al Najaz's hopes in that direction by refusing to take part, he would be perfectly capable of just moving on to something else.

"In fact, the princes are assuming that this plan he's engaged in now has been in the making for years, too. Clearly he has a taste for conspiracy."

Talk like this made her nervous. "What kind of plan could it be? And what will he do with the disaffected Cup Companion when he gets hold of him?" she won-

dered, aloud stroking his powerful, naked shoulder and
wishing it didn't have to be Jaf. Wishing hard that she
hadn't paused in front of that painting of Sheikh Daud
on the night of the Grand Reception.

"It may never come to that, Lisbet. You're the one
who will be in danger. Please don't do anything foolishly brave. Don't try to manipulate him into saying
something incriminating. If he gets suspicious he may
search you, and that would ruin everything. Just let
him pay you off and go. I'll handle whatever comes
after. Don't worry. Promise?"

She heaved a breath. "All right."

He kissed her. "Ready to start?"

A few hours later, they stood over their "favourite"
roulette table, while Lisbet, charmingly female, all but
ordered Jaf to play her lucky number. It was a last-
ditch attempt to restore his fortunes. She had lost all
track of the amount they had blown tonight. It was
simply unbelievable.

She was looking dramatically beautiful, in a clinging metallic gold dress that hugged every curve to her
ankles. It was slit to above the knee at the back. With
it she wore gold strappy stilettos and no stockings on
her tanned legs.

She was draped with emeralds, from the emerald-
and-diamond star in her smoothly flowing hair to a
tiny emerald-and-gold ankle chain. In between she
wore earrings, a pendant, upper arm bracelet and two
rings, all in the same dark, glowing green set off with
flashing diamonds.

Her excited eyes flashed green fire, her tanned skin
was smooth and bore all the signs of total pampering.

"Kiss me for luck," Jaf said, as he stacked all his

remaining chips on number twenty-two. In a black tuxedo, with a white burnoose thrown back over his shoulders like a cape, he looked like a nineteenth-century rake.

There was a glint in his eyes that melted her where she stood. He could always do it to her. However angry he might be underneath, when Jaf turned on the charm, she was jelly. Sweet, and wobbly, and ready to be gobbled up.

"Kiss me," he commanded, as the little ball began its fatal journey around the wheel.

The luck he wanted wasn't to win, of course, but to lose. They had made a show of this being his last hope. Everyone at the table knew that Jaf was down to his last barakati, and Lisbet had encouraged him to risk everything he had left on her intuition.

"I don't know how we'll get home!" he had warned her, but Lisbet had waved blithely and said, "On our winnings!"

And he had let the foolhardy bet stand.

Now he dragged her into his embrace with one strong, hungry arm, and his eyes gazed into hers from point-blank range. Behind them the wheel whirred and the ball spun, around and around.

"Kiss me, Lisbet," he murmured, "and tell me you love me."

He didn't mean it. It was all for show, but it would be a relief to say it. "I love you," she breathed.

His mouth covered hers with a rough passion that made the world disappear. Lisbet felt herself spinning as helplessly as the little white ball.

"I love you," he whispered when he lifted his mouth.

Behind them there was a collective gasp from the

crowd around the table, and they remembered and broke apart and turned to see their luck.

"Twelve," intoned the croupier.

"Noooo!" Lisbet cried in dismay. Jaf was silent, but she felt him stiffen in well-acted dismay.

The rake came out and inexorably dragged the massively stacked chips on number twenty-two across the green board. They fell into the maw where the house profits went, with a rattling *thunk.*

Jaf muttered a quiet curse and finished off the champagne in his gold-traced flute glass. "Right," he said, slightly unsteadily, setting the glass down on the edge of the roulette table. "That's the end of me. Let's go."

He took her arm and turned around, but Lisbet snatched her elbow away from his touch with a laugh. "You can't quit now!" she cried. "Our luck is turning, can't you see? Twelve, that's just one digit away from twenty-two! One more try, Jaf."

He resisted, she implored. The other players began to shift away in discomfort. "Come on," she cried at last. "For me, just one more little try?"

He was getting annoyed. "There is no more," he told her. "That's the last of it. You'll have to sell one of your trinkets if you want to play, darling." He flicked the emerald at her ear.

Staff of the casino were hovering, hoping to quiet them without taking more extreme measures. A bouncer was making a carefully unaggressive approach. A Cup Companion was still a Cup Companion, and besides, Jafar al Hamzeh was in peak condition, and even drunk his reflexes were probably lightning.

"I didn't realize you were such a coward!" Lisbet cried. "I thought you were an adventurer."

"Shhh!" he complained. "Come on, darling, don't make a fuss. We'll go home now."

"I'm not going anywhere! I'm staying right here! Are you going to place a bet or not?"

"Not," said Jaf, swaying slightly, but determined. "Have to borrow from Gazi as it is. You've cleaned me out, baby."

Lisbet's eyes and mouth opened in shocked outrage. "I cleaned you out? *I* cleaned you out? How dare you say a thing like that to me?"

The staff moved closer, the volume of her voice feeding their determination. Lisbet Raine, previously so fun-loving and good-natured, was starting to sound like a housewife being cheated in the *souk*. Her voice climbed, and the green eyes looked dangerous.

"Miss Raine," one murmured bravely, foolishly attempting to grasp her arm.

"Take your hands off me!" the actress cried, snatching her arm away so violently that they all watched fascinated for her breasts to come tumbling out of the low-cut dress. There was a collective sigh when it did not happen.

She was still shrieking at Jaf as members of the staff herded the couple to the door of the room, and finally she gave in to their force majeure.

"Don't bother to come with me!" she cried to Jaf. "You've seen the last of me!" And with one final imprecation, she stormed out.

Jafar al Hamzeh, his eyes dark with shock, straightened his suit jacket, twitched his burnoose over his shoulders, nodded elegantly at those who stood staring, and followed his lady love.

* * *

"I will give you an address," said the voice she recognized. "Come at once."

In the darkened limousine, Lisbet held her cell phone to her ear and took a deep breath. They hadn't been sure what course he would take. He might easily have put her off at this point, promising her a reward that never arrived.

"All right," she said.

"Tell your driver to take you to Mukaafa Road, the corner nearest the Jamaa al Fannun *souk*. From the casino it will take you no more than fifteen minutes. Someone will meet you there."

Lisbet disconnected with a steady hand. Now that it was happening, she felt very cool.

"Mukaafa Road?" the driver repeated. Behind the concealing keffiyeh was Arif al Rashid.

"The corner near the Crafts Market. Someone will meet me."

The Cup Companion nodded. "Thank you." The limousine swung out of the casino parking lot into the light traffic along the coastal highway, and headed back into the capital.

At her feet in the darkened car, Gazi said, "Let's test your mike, Lisbet."

"There is one small thing I require of you, Miss Raine," said Yadeth al Najaz. "Would you be so kind as to call Jafar al Hamzeh and ask him to meet you here."

His voice was flat with disdain. She was reaping the reward of traitors throughout time—the contempt of those whom the betrayal benefits.

"Call him! Are you kidding me? I'm not going to call him," Lisbet exclaimed. Her overt defiance was a cover for real dismay. What did they want Jaf here for? What were they going to do to him? Were the princes all wrong about this? Was it a personal vendetta against Jaf after all?

"I am afraid you must."

"There's no *must* about any of this," she told him angrily.

*"Laa ikraa,"* the man murmured. "No compulsion, Miss Raine, but your reward depends upon it."

"That isn't what you told me. That wasn't the deal. You never said Jaf had to know what I was doing."

She was fighting for time to think. A dozen different scenarios passed through her imagination. Would they make him a fake suicide, saying he had been unhinged by her rejection? Stage a domestic murder? Have him stabbed in one of the less salubrious streets of this neighbourhood?

"But sadly, it is necessary. It is part of the shock treatment I spoke of. Only when he fully realizes the emptiness of his way of life and the untrustworthiness of the Westerners he so loves to mingle with will the full shock take effect. Call him, Miss Raine."

"No." Lisbet leaned back against the cushions on the divan and crossed her arms. She thought of the Cup Companions, who were listening to this from the car, and felt their urgency. Of course they would want her to do as Yadeth al Najaz said. They were Cup Companions. No doubt, as far as they were concerned, risking their lives in the service of their princes was no more than a duty.

But she was a woman who loved a man. How could she summon Jaf into unknown danger?

Yadeth al Najaz smiled. "You know how to bargain," he said with false admiration. He nodded to the other man in the room, a younger man who might be his son. He was the one who had met her at the car and escorted her half a block to a small apartment building. Now he went into another room and returned. A silver suitcase was lifted onto the low table between them. With a calm smile Yadeth al Najaz clicked open the locks, lifted the lid, turned the case to face her.

It was filled with cash. She bit back her reaction.

"This case contains one million American dollars, Miss Raine. It is for you."

She couldn't help her startled intake of breath then, but didn't move from her adamant posture. "Real, or counterfeit?" she asked cynically.

He inclined his head with respect for her business acumen. "You see for yourself, they are all used notes."

With a knowing grin, she leaned forward and carelessly reached out to riffle through the neat piles of hundred-dollar bills, making sure it was all money. She sat back, flicking her hand.

"What good is cash going to do me? People ask questions, you know, when someone walks into a bank with a boatload of used American dollars."

"Arrangements will be made for you at a bank here," he said. "Now, Miss Raine. I know you have your mobile phone with you. Please use it."

She stared at him for a long moment, miming sulky resistance while her brain whirled, looking for a solution. With the phone in the little gold mesh handbag was the transmitter for the remote microphone that was taped under her breast. It was inexpertly disguised as a mirror case.

Yadeth al Najaz's assistant was now sitting beside

her on the sofa. How much danger was she in, if they realized she had set them up? Yadeth al Najaz might not guess that they already knew his name. Might they hope to escape by killing her and fleeing?

If she failed now, everything was lost. The princes knew who he was, but they had no idea what he planned, and no evidence to bring this evil man to justice. It was up to her, and no one else. The future of the Barakat Emirates might be in her hands.

But so was her own future, and Jaf's.

Lisbet heaved a breath. "All right!" she exclaimed mulishly, picking up the little gold bag and snapping it carelessly open. "But it's not exactly fair, is it?"

"What a very English sentiment, Miss Raine. Life is seldom fair. That is why religions inevitably promise justice in the other world."

# Thirteen

## ——

"**I** don't understand," Jaf said, glancing from Yadeth al Najaz to the case full of money and back to Lisbet again. She sat on the sofa, her arms crossed, looking defiant. "How are you involved in this, *Sadin al Qasr?*"

"It is simple, Your Excellency. Betrayal always is. Miss Raine brought you to us for a price. Isn't it so, Miss Raine?"

"Call it what you like!" she sneered. "Why would you pay a million dollars for a meeting with Jaf? All anyone has to do is book an appointment. But if Jaf wants to believe it, he can."

Jaf frowned. "A million dollars? Why did you wish to organize a meeting in this way, *Sadin al Qasr?*"

"Ah, but it was more than a meeting, wasn't it? You agreed to bring him to ruin, did you not?" the old man said to Lisbet.

"Lisbet?" Jaf whispered disbelievingly.

"Believe that and you'll believe anything!" she snapped. "Now, can I please get out of here?"

She made to stand up, but Yadeth al Najaz held up a hand. "Not yet, please. You see where you are, Excellency. Did you think she loved you? I bought that love for a million dollars. You have spent much more than that on her, I am sure." He spread his hands helplessly. "But women are such changeable creatures.

"And you have lost everything, after all. What will be next? Miss Raine had to ask herself, as a practical woman. Her lovely jewels? Women such as she do not like to make sacrifices of that nature."

Jaf was looking stunned. "Lisbet, is it true? But why? I love you! I would do anything for you. You know it."

Lisbet sniffed and turned her head. "I didn't know it was going to turn out like this," she said sulkily. "It's not my fault you didn't win."

Jaf sank forward and put his head in his hands. "I've drunk too much. I can't think straight. What is it you want, *Sadin?*"

"Only to help you."

"You aren't leaving me, Lisbet? You can't. I can't live without you!" Jaf said, in a desperate voice that made her heart beat hard. Oh, if only that were true!

"Don't worry, Your Excellency. If you play your cards right, you can still win. Miss Raine will have no reason to leave you if you win, will she?"

"What do you mean?"

"I want you to make a phone call. One phone call. If you do that—" he flicked the silver suitcase "—you may take this money and go."

"Wait a minute!" Lisbet cried angrily. "You said that was mine already!"

"But we have already agreed, haven't we, that life is not fair?" Yadeth al Najaz turned to Jaf.

"Make the call and you may consider this—" he flicked the cash contemptuously "—a mere down payment. Your lifestyle will be guaranteed from now on. Your losses restored to you. How many millions have you thrown away? Never mind, Excellency. They will be yours again."

Lisbet sat a little forward in unconscious interest.

"You see?" said al Najaz.

Jaf rubbed his eyes, as if trying to clear his head. "What phone call?"

A card was placed on the table before him.

"Call this number. Ask for this man."

Jaf's eyes narrowed as he read the scrawled name. "I know this name. The man is a journalist," he said. "An English newspaper."

"You will tell him you want an immediate meeting with him. And give him this address."

Jaf tossed the card onto the table with easy contempt. "No."

Yadeth al Najaz smiled and signalled his younger henchman. "In that case—"

The other man closed the suitcase, snapped the locks, stood up.

"Wait a minute!" Lisbet shrieked in alarm. "That's mine!"

"If His Excellency makes the call, it is yours."

Jaf waved an arrogant hand. "Take it away. We don't want your money."

"Wait a minute, darling," Lisbet said quickly. "It won't hurt to ask what it's all about, will it?"

"Nobody uses bribes and blackmail to achieve any legitimate purpose," Jaf told her grandly. "Now, let's get out of here."

She smiled seductively at him. "I'm sure you're right, but at least let's ask." She turned to Yadeth al Najaz. The younger man hesitated, holding the shiny aluminum case as if uncertain what to do. "What's the call about, actually?"

"It is of no import, Miss Raine," al Najaz said, waving his henchman away. "If he will not do it, he will not. Someone else will be more willing."

"Just a minute, I said!" Lisbet shouted. All three men looked at her. "What is the call about? What does Jaf have to say to him?"

"Nothing beyond what I have already said. He asks the man to come here. Then you can go, with the money. And there will be more to follow."

Lisbet's eyes narrowed. "What are you going to do to the man? Is he going to be hurt in any way?"

The old man laughed. "On the contrary. He will be given the scoop of his career!"

Lisbet sat back, blinking. "Oh! Well, that's not bad, is it?" She turned to Jaf. "You can do that, can't you, darling?"

Jaf shook his head suspiciously. "What scoop? What story, *Sadin?*"

"I wish you two would stop calling each other by your titles in that ridiculous way!" Lisbet interjected. They ignored her.

"Nothing that nearly concerns you, or yours, I assure you."

Lisbet smiled and tilted her head. "You could do it, couldn't you, Jaf? It's enough money to be going on with, isn't it? And if you don't, you said yourself you'd have to ask Gazi for funds. I know you won't like that, and neither will he.''

"I want to know what the story is," Jaf said doggedly.

Lisbet sank down beside him, her thigh touching his. His body heat burned her, and for the first time since her arrival she felt how deeply her system thrilled to the danger they were in.

She stroked a lock of hair back from his forehead. "What difference does it make? A story's a story, whoever calls the journalist. It's not going to go away because you don't make the call."

He grasped her upper arm, and she shivered at the power in his hold. The side-by-side presence of danger and safety made her blood rush through her like electricity.

"Lisbet, don't."

"Do you love me, Jaf?" she asked, and suddenly her voice quivered on tears, and the question was real.

"Lisbet—"

"Do you?"

"You know I love you," he said roughly, gazing into her eyes, and to her starved soul it sounded like the truth. She closed her eyes, smiling. It was an act, but she was glad she had heard it one last time. Something to remember.

"I love you, Jaf. I always have."

They were still for a moment, gazing at each other. Behind them, Yadeth al Najaz cleared his throat.

"Please do this for me," she whispered.

He put her to one side and stood up. "Let's get out of here."

"Jaf!" she cried, a woman playing her trump card. "If you leave now, I'll never speak to you again."

He turned and glared down at her. "You will," he said, trying for firmness.

She picked up her mobile. "Make the call for me, Jaf. Never mind him." She nodded towards the old man. "Do it for my sake."

"You sold me out," he muttered, like a man who has lost his footing and knows he will not regain it. "I know damned well you'll walk out on me as soon as you get your hands on that money."

"No," she cried softly, as he took the phone. "No, never, Jaf. How can I ever leave you? Please!"

Jaf, with the self-loathing of a man driven to do what he should not for an end he knows he will never achieve, took the phone and made the call.


"It was a majestic plan, Lord," Jaf explained to the three princes and several Cup Companions as they sat again in the King's Pavilion.

"Tell us," said Prince Karim.

"The file I was to pass on to the journalist documents a complete production line for heroin, from the seed all the way through to the distribution of the final product in Western Europe.

"All that was needed was someone to link that complete body of evidence with the Princes of Barakat, to say that you were producing and selling heroin to the West to boost your export revenues.

"That was why a Cup Companion was necessary. Someone whose word alone would be compelling evidence."

"But you did not give the file to the journalist?"

"No, Lord. Fortunately, both my microphone and Lisbet's continued to transmit throughout the evening. The task force in the street was able to detain the journalist and send in a ringer. Yadeth al Najaz fell for it.''

"How do investigations stand now, Hashem?" Rafi asked.

The Cup Companion cleared his throat. "Poppy fields have been discovered in the Noor Mountains, just where the documentation showed, on the border between Central and Eastern Barakat. The refinery also exists. So much we know. We are moving very carefully, Lord, so as to retain the element of surprise. We expect to make arrests within twelve hours.''

Lisbet and Jaf walked along the beach under starlight.

"So Ramiz is coming home now?"

"Soon, we hope. The princes were very complimentary about you, Lisbet."

"What did they say?" Lisbet asked.

"They asked me to pass on their deep gratitude and admiration for your courage. Of course, that is not the end of it. They made it clear that they intend to reward you, but want to know first what you would consider a suitable recompense.''

"Oh!" She hadn't thought of that.

"They've asked me to sound you out. The sky is the limit, I think, Lisbet.''

"But what sort of thing do they mean?"

"You might ask for property here or abroad, or money, or an honorary title, I suppose. They are very determined that your reward should fit your courage. Of course, they will see you and express their gratitude in person.

"The proceedings in Yadeth al Najaz's place were taped, by the way, and the princes have listened to the entire scene with great interest. They are deeply impressed with your abilities, and Prince Rafi suggested that, if we could not convince you to join the police, you might undertake to set up a permanent British-Barakati film unit, with the aim of producing more joint productions.''

Lisbet laughed and shook her head incredulously. "I can't believe this is happening!" She looked up at the ever-magical night sky. "You're right. It's not the same sky at all as the one in London. I think I'm on a totally different planet."

Jaf laughed lightly. "You have time to get used to it. There is no rush to make up your mind. Think it over, Lisbet. This moment may affect all the rest of your life, if you choose wisely."

She kicked at the wet sand, exposing the paler sand beneath, and dug her toes into the cool softness. "I don't think that the princes have the power to give me what I want," she murmured.

Jaf raised startled eyebrows. "I would be very surprised if they did not. What is it you want?"

"It's something only you could give me," she said, her heart beating hard enough to kill her. "And I doubt you'd be willing."

"If it's the piece called the Concubine's Tears you wish for, it is yours, Lisbet. Do you think me so ungenerous?"

"Not that."

He frowned. "What, then?"

She looked up into his shadowed face and felt how much more dangerous this moment was than the one in which they had played their game for the traitor. Now, truly, she felt she risked everything. Life and limb was nothing compared to the risk to her heart.

"I want to hear you say you love me again," she whispered. "The way you did in front of Yadeth al Najaz. Only…I'd like you to mean it."

His mouth tightened, and her heart sank. She had known it would be too much to hope that the adventure they had been through would have softened him, but still the death of hope hurt.

"And what would you do with such a reward, Lisbet?"

She shook her head, because tears were burning her throat too painfully for speech. "Never mind," she managed.

She turned away, but he caught her shoulders in a hard hold and kept her there. "What would you do with such a rebirth of love, Lisbet? Run from it again? If I loved you, what then?"

She looked up, too scared to hope, too hungry to despair. Her eyes were bright with tears.

"I've changed, Jaf. I've learned so much about myself, about life…about love. If the princes were willing, I'd ask them—to let me marry one of their Cup Companions."

"Do you love me, Lisbet?" he asked harshly.

"Yes, *yes,* I love you. I adore you. I didn't know it before, because I was so afraid. But I've loved you from the beginning, just the way you always said, Jaf. You were right, it was magical and special, and there will never be anyone in the world for me but you.

"It's killing me that I didn't find it out until I'd lost your love. Please try to love me again, Jaf! Please believe that that love may still be alive in you, underneath. Please try to find that love in your heart, be-

178 THE PLAYBOY SHEIKH

cause I want to marry you and have children with you,
and lots of grandchildren. I want them to learn that
service is the duty of privilege, and grow up to be Cup
Companions like their father.

"But most of all, I want to love you and be loved
by you. Jaf, please say it's not hopeless. Please say I
haven't killed your love forever!"

"This is what I have been waiting to hear from you,
Lisbet," he whispered, his hands clasping her upper
arms, pulling her close.

She gasped, feeling as if one of the stars had fallen
to earth and hit her. "What?" she breathed.

"Am I a weakling, whose love dies with one small
blow?" he growled. "Can you believe such lies?" His
arms wrapped her and he pulled her close. "Kill my
love? You didn't kill my love for so much as a minute,
my beloved, my wife!"

Then his mouth covered hers and her body sank into
his, and they tasted joy.


"Why did you tell me it was too late for us?" she
protested later, as they lay looking out at the sea and
the stars.

Jaf smiled. "You see, I had a problem. If I chased
you, I only proved your fears, that I would overrule
your real needs for the sake of my own. The more I
told you I loved you, the less chance there was of
winning you.

"When I came back to the Barakat Emirates last
spring having failed to bring you with me, I understood that I needed a strategy. And the strategy I chose
was to let you believe that I no longer loved you."

"But you said, *It's too late for us,*" Lisbet protested, in remembered pain.

"Yes. I thought that it was the way to get you to recognize love and throw away fear. If I pounced on you, I would lose you again. Like a wild animal watching for its prey, I had to wait until you came out of hiding all the way, by yourself. Then there would be no way back for you.

"But it was more difficult than I imagined."

"Was it?"

"I could not resist making love to you. It was not part of my strategy, but I was powerless to resist. So I told you it was a purely physical passion. And you were foolish enough to believe it."

He smiled at her, melting her heart.

"So your anger was an act?" she said, lifting her head.

He kissed her ruthlessly again. "It was no act. I was very deeply angry with you, but I was also in love and fighting to keep myself in check. It was not easy to be around you and pretend indifference. But I had one advantage."

"Which was?"

"I was already forced to live one lie. That made it easier for me. I had to act the part of a fool. Whenever I was in danger of telling you the truth, there was always the necessity to go to the casino to help me overcome it. And the fact that you could not sway me would always convince you that I didn't love you, no matter how dangerously I had slipped."

"And now?"

"And now, my strategy has finally paid off. You have left fear behind, and there is no way back," he promised her, in a tone that thrilled her.

She kissed him, and his strong arms wrapped her, protecting, possessing. Her heart leapt.

Lisbet rolled over on her back. "And are we going to get married?"

Jaf rose onto one elbow above her. His eyelids drooped and his hand slipped up over the tender throat. "You know we are," he said. "And very soon. I have waited for too long, Lisbet. I will not wait much longer to call you my wife."

"Will you promise, as the princes have, never to take another wife?" she teased.

"You are behind the times. It is against the law here, except in exceptional circumstances."

He stroked her flank, her side, her arm. His hand caught her upper arm in a firm clasp and he drew her up a little for his kiss. "But even if it were not against the law," he said, "there will never be another woman for me, Lisbet."

"You know," she said later, sighing in satisfaction, "there's one thing I've realized about myself in all this."

"What is that?"

"That I didn't really accept that it was over when I broke up with you. I think I was testing you, or something. I think that's why I kept sending you those cheques. Really, I was trying to stir you to action."

Jaf lay back with a little laugh, as though she had hit him. "Of course!" he exclaimed. "Why didn't I see that? Months of misery might have been spared."

"Were you miserable? But you never tried to see me, never called, never came after me. I really thought you'd forgotten me when I came to do the movie. And when you didn't visit Gazi and Anna in that first week, I was sure of it."

"I didn't forget you for one day," he assured her. "One hour."

"But—you didn't do anything about it, either. If I hadn't got this film when would we ever have met again?"

Now he was laughing gently. He lay back and drew her onto his chest, stroking her hair and all the length of her back with a firm, possessive hand that thrilled her.

"Lisbet, did you never guess? Never suspect? Not once?" he demanded, amused.

"Suspect what?"

"Masoud al Badi is an old, old friend, Lisbet. He was looking for financing for his film. He failed to get it off the ground last year and he had put the project on hold."

"No!" Lisbet cried. She broke out of his hold to sit bolt upright.

"You didn't! You couldn't have! Oh, Jaf, don't tell me—you mean that newspaper story was *right?*"

Jaf shouted with laughter. "Of course it was right! Who do you think was feeding all those stories to the press from the beginning, if not Gazi?"

*"You bought my way into Masoud's film?"*

"He did tell me it was no deal if he didn't think you were up to the weight," he said.

"Jaf, you *monster!*" she cried. "How can you laugh about it? How could you *do* it? Oh, my God! How humiliating! Who knows about this? Does everybody know except me?"

He was still laughing. "But Masoud loves you. He says he only wishes he'd cast me as the sultan. We would burn up the screen, he says, as we did on the beach."

"I was so right about you!" she cried. "It's the apartment all over again, isn't it? Manipulating me for my own good, I suppose you call it! But it's really just—"

"But you can't have it both ways, Lisbet! You can't complain that I never lifted a finger to win you in one breath and then in the next complain because I did!"

"But you didn't have to do it *this* way!"

"What else would have brought you in my way? If I had come to London, you'd have run away screaming."

"But—"

He caught her head between his two hands. "No, my darling, I am sure we will have many, many enjoyable arguments in future, but tonight I refuse to fight with you. Tonight is for love, Lisbet. Tonight we celebrate the mystery of how, out of all the stars in the universe, you and I found each other."

# Epilogue

***Actress Honoured in Barakat Emirates***

Lisbet Raine, the British actress, and her fiancé Sheikh Jafar al Hamzeh, are to receive the country's highest honour from the Princes of the Barakat Emirates, it was disclosed today. The "playboy" Cup Companion and his bride have each individually been awarded the coveted title *Qalb al Maliki,* or King's Heart.

The honour is a rare one, historically awarded for service above and beyond the high degree of service normally expected from a Cup Companion in the Barakat Emirates. It is rare for the award to be made to anyone not a Cup Companion. Miss Raine is the first woman, and the first foreigner, so honoured.

The reputation of the renegade sheikh, who until

recently appeared to be on the brink of being stripped of his Cup Companion status, seems to be fully restored by the announcement.

The sheikh is widely rumoured to have taken an active part in the recent highly publicized cracking of a heroin-producing ring in the country.

Sources say that it is impossible that Miss Raine would have been given the award merely as a reflection of her fiancé's services.

Palace sources, however, refuse to disclose the precise reason for the awards.

*     *     *     *     *

*Desire®*

MAN OF THE MONTH

January 2002
**THE REDEMPTION OF JEFFERSON CADE**
**#1411 by BJ James**

MEN of Belle Terre

Don't miss the fifth book in BJ James' exciting miniseries featuring irresistible heroes from Belle Terre, South Carolina.

February 2002
**THE PLAYBOY SHEIKH**
**#1417 by Alexandra Sellers**

SONS OF THE DESERT

Alexandra Sellers continues her sensual miniseries about powerful sheikhs and the women they're destined to love.

March 2002
**BILLIONAIRE BACHELORS: STONE**
**#1423 by Anne Marie Winston**

Bestselling author Anne Marie Winston's Billionaire Bachelors prove they're not immune to the power of love.

# MAN OF THE MONTH

Some men are made for lovin'—and you're sure to love these three upcoming men of the month!

*Available at your favorite retail outlet.*

**Silhouette®**

*Where love comes alive™*

Visit Silhouette at www.eHarlequin.com          SDMOM02Q1

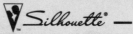

# This Mother's Day
# Give Your Mom
 ## A Royal Treat

Win a fabulous one-week vacation in
Puerto Rico for you and your mother at
the luxurious Inter-Continental San Juan
Resort & Casino. The prize includes round
trip airfare for two, breakfast daily and a
mother and daughter day of beauty
at the beachfront hotel's spa.

## INTER·CONTINENTAL
### San Juan
#### RESORT & CASINO

## Here's all you have to do:

Tell us in 100 words or less how your
mother helped with the romance in your
life. It may be a story about your engagement,
wedding or those boyfriends when you were
a teenager or any other romantic advice
from your mother. The entry will be judged
based on its originality, emotionally
compelling nature and sincerity.
See official rules on following page.

### Send your entry to:
## Mother's Day Contest

| **In Canada** | **In U.S.A.** |
|---|---|
| P.O. Box 637 | P.O. Box 9076 |
| Fort Erie, Ontario | 3010 Walden Ave. |
| L2A 5X3 | Buffalo, NY |
| | 14269-9076 |

## Or enter online at www.eHarlequin.com

All entries must be postmarked by April 1, 2002.
Winner will be announced May 1, 2002. Contest open to
Canadian and U.S. residents who are 18 years of age and older.
No purchase necessary to enter. Void where prohibited.

PRROY

Two ways to enter:

• **Via The Internet:** Log on to the Harlequin romance website (www.eHarlequin.com) anytime beginning 12:01 a.m. E.S.T., January 1, 2002 through 11:59 p.m. E.S.T., April 1, 2002 and follow the directions displayed on-line to enter your name, address (including zip code), e-mail address and in 100 words or fewer, describe how your mother helped with the romance in your life.

• **Via Mail:** Handprint (or type) on an 8 1/2" x 11" plain piece of paper, your name, address (including zip code) and e-mail address (if you have one), and in 100 words or fewer, describe how your mother helped with the romance in your life. Mail your entry via first-class mail to: Harlequin Mother's Day Contest 2216, (in the U.S.) P.O. Box 9076, Buffalo, NY 14269-9076; (in Canada) P.O. Box 637, Fort Erie, Ontario, Canada L2A 5X3.

For eligibility, entries must be submitted either through a completed Internet transmission or postmarked no later than 11:59 p.m. E.S.T., April 1, 2002 (mail-in entries must be received by April 9, 2002). Limit one entry per person, household address and e-mail address. On-line and/or mailed entries received from persons residing in geographic areas in which entry is not permissible will be disqualified.

Entries will be judged by a panel of judges, consisting of members of the Harlequin editorial, marketing and public relations staff using the following criteria:
> • Originality - 50%
> • Emotional Appeal - 25%
> • Sincerity - 25%

In the event of a tie, duplicate prizes will be awarded. Decisions of the judges are final.

Prize: A 6-night/7-day stay for two at the Inter-Continental San Juan Resort & Casino, including round-trip coach air transportation from gateway airport nearest winner's home (approximate retail value: $4,000). Prize includes breakfast daily and a mother and daughter day of beauty at the beachfront hotel's spa. Prize consists of only those items listed as part of the prize. Prize is valued in U.S. currency.

All entries become the property of Torstar Corp. and will not be returned. No responsibility is assumed for lost, late, illegible, incomplete, inaccurate, non-delivered or misdirected mail or misdirected e-mail, for technical, hardware or software failures of any kind, lost or unavailable network connections, or failed, incomplete, garbled or delayed computer transmission or any human error which may occur in the receipt or processing of the entries in this Contest.

Contest open only to residents of the U.S. (except Colorado) and Canada, who are 18 years of age or older and is void wherever prohibited by law; all applicable laws and regulations apply. Any litigation within the Province of Quebec respecting the conduct or organization of a publicity contest may be submitted to the Régie des alcools, des courses et des jeux for a ruling. Any litigation respecting the awarding of a prize may be submitted to the Régie des alcools, des courses et des jeux only for the purpose of helping the parties reach a settlement. Employees and immediate family members of Torstar Corp. and D.L. Blair, Inc., their affiliates, subsidiaries and all other agencies, entities and persons connected with the use, marketing or conduct of this Contest are not eligible to enter. Taxes on prize are the sole responsibility of winner. Acceptance of any prize offered constitutes permission to use winner's name, photograph or other likeness for the purposes of advertising, trade and promotion on behalf of Torstar Corp., its affiliates and subsidiaries without further compensation to the winner, unless prohibited by law.

Winner will be determined no later than April 15, 2002 and be notified by mail. Winner will be required to sign and return an Affidavit of Eligibility form within 15 days after winner notification. Non-compliance within that time period may result in disqualification and an alternate winner may be selected. Winner of trip must execute a Release of Liability prior to ticketing and must possess required travel documents (e.g. Passport, photo ID) where applicable. Travel must be completed within 12 months of selection and is subject to traveling companion completing and returning a Release of Liability prior to travel; and hotel and flight accommodations availability. Certain restrictions and blackout dates may apply. No substitution of prize permitted by winner. Torstar Corp. and D.L. Blair, Inc., their parents, affiliates, and subsidiaries are not responsible for errors in printing or electronic presentation of Contest, or entries. In the event of printing or other errors which may result in unintended prize values or duplication of prizes, all affected entries shall be null and void. If for any reason the Internet portion of the Contest is not capable of running as planned, including infection by computer virus, bugs, tampering, unauthorized intervention, fraud, technical failures, or any other causes beyond the control of Torstar Corp. which corrupt or affect the administration, secrecy, fairness, integrity or proper conduct of the Contest, Torstar Corp. reserves the right, at its sole discretion, to disqualify any individual who tampers with the entry process and to cancel, terminate, modify or suspend the Contest or the Internet portion thereof. In the event the Internet portion must be terminated a notice will be posted on the website and all entries received prior to termination will be judged in accordance with these rules. In the event of a dispute regarding an on-line entry, the entry will be deemed submitted by the authorized holder of the e-mail account submitted at the time of entry. Authorized account holder is defined as the natural person who is assigned to an e-mail address by an Internet access provider, on-line service provider or other organization that is responsible for arranging e-mail address for the domain associated with the submitted e-mail address. Torstar Corp. and/or D.L. Blair Inc. assumes no responsibility for any computer injury or damage related to or resulting from accessing and/or downloading any sweepstakes material. Rules are subject to any requirements/ limitations imposed by the FCC. **Purchase or acceptance of a product offer does not improve your chances of winning.**

For winner's name (available after May 1, 2002), send a self-addressed, stamped envelope to: Harlequin Mother's Day Contest Winners 2216, P.O. Box 4200 Blair, NE 68009-4200 or you may access the www.eHarlequin.com Web site through June 3, 2002.

Contest sponsored by Torstar Corp., P.O. Box 9042, Buffalo, NY 14269-9042.

**Silhouette® Desire®**

## presents

**DYNASTIES: THE CONNELLYS**

A brand-new miniseries about the Connellys of Chicago, a wealthy, powerful American family tied by blood to the royal family of the island kingdom of Altaria. They're wealthy, powerful and rocked by scandal, betrayal…and passion!

Look for a whole year of glamorous and utterly romantic tales in 2002:

January: **TALL, DARK & ROYAL by Leanne Banks**

February: **MATERNALLY YOURS by Kathie DeNosky**

March: **THE SHEIKH TAKES A BRIDE by Caroline Cross**

April: **THE SEAL'S SURRENDER by Maureen Child**

May: **PLAIN JANE & DOCTOR DAD by Kate Little**

June: **AND THE WINNER GETS…MARRIED! by Metsy Hingle**

July: **THE ROYAL & THE RUNAWAY BRIDE by Kathryn Jensen**

August: **HIS E-MAIL ORDER WIFE by Kristi Gold**

September: **THE SECRET BABY BOND by Cindy Gerard**

October: **CINDERELLA'S CONVENIENT HUSBAND by Katherine Garbera**

November: **EXPECTING…AND IN DANGER by Eileen Wilks**

December: **CHEROKEE MARRIAGE DARE by Sheri WhiteFeather**

**Silhouette®**

*Where love comes alive™*